All Creation Sings

Children's Stories
for the
Golden Age

All Creation Sings
Children's Stories
for the
Golden Age

Sharan Shively

Illustrations by
Sharan Shively and Valerie Tarrant

Happily Ever After Press

Published by Happily Ever After Press
© Copyright 2004 by Happily Ever After Press.
All rights reserved. No part of this book may be used
or reproduced in any manner whatsoever without
written permission except in the case of brief quota-
tions embodied in critical articles and reviews.

For information, write:
Happily Ever After Press
P.O. Box 3268
Lisle, IL 60532

Illustrations for Attitude of Gratitude, Bob Too,
Catkin, Little Lizard (beginning illustration),
Merlin Mouse's Merry Christmas 1 & 2, and
Secret Love by Valerie Tarrant.
Cover and other illustrations by Sharan Shively.
Book Design and Layout by Isabel Wolf.
Editing: Kathryn Kruger, Larry Levin, Sam Pletcher,
Debbie Purdy, and Valerie Tarrant.

Printed on recycled paper.

ISBN 0-615-11918-2

Dedication

I dedicate this book to my beloved teachers,
Sant Kirpal Singh Ji Maharaj,
Sant Darshan Singh Ji Maharaj, and
Sant Rajinder Singh Ji Maharaj,
because I owe my life to their kindness.

Table of Contents

Holly, Hearth & Home — Holiday Stories

Earth, Air, Fire & Water — Learning Love Stories

Introduction

In her luminous children's book, *All Creation Sings*, Sharan Shively conveys a vision of a new age, a Golden Age, wherein we can learn the art of living together in peace and mutual love. Ranging from fantasy to fable, Sharan's stories offer good advice for leading a spiritual life in a confusing world.

Sharan refers to many traditions in her writing, such as European fairy tale, animal fabliaux, and Native American myth, but to whatever world Sharan may transport us, the journey is the same. Many of her heroes and heroines travel through strange forests and lands, but ultimately discover that no matter what difficulty they encounter in life, to find their solution they must first turn within. The journey to one's heart is a far greater pilgrimage than any path they may travel in the world.

In *All Creation Sings*, we meet delightful characters who befriend us in their struggles to find wisdom and the light of truth and love. In the story, "The Snow Maiden," Grayse discovers that her ancestors' selfish actions have created an eternity of winter in their world. Only by committing acts of kindness will her people be able to break the spell and prepare for the coming of spring. In the tale "Death, the Maiden and Mikhail," Glynnis learns that though death can not always be avoided, life continues in the eternal realm of spirit. In the Native American fable "Back from the Stars," a young Ojibway learns that forgiveness takes strength, but is one of the greatest gifts we can bestow on others. And in the story "Catkin," an entertaining and self-satisfied cat learns that the journey to love is not as easy as it first may seem.

The young heroes or heroines are often guided to meditate. By turning within they receive answers to important questions, learn to see themselves and others with more clarity, and discover how to connect with an inner Light that fills them with a sense of extraordinary love and peace. Sharan's characters discover this truth in different ways. Sometimes they will speak with a divine presence — an angel, a wise old man, or even a voice whose wisdom eases all doubt and suffering. At other times her characters will learn that the qualities of courage, faith and love — those qualities we often seek in others — exist already inside of themselves. And, like a valuable treasure that has been discarded or lost, through meditation they rediscover the jewel of compassion buried within their heart.

Sharan brings a new dimension to the art of storytelling by showing us that her characters' achievements are not determined by worldly gain or prestige. Instead, their successes are measured by their capacity for generosity and kindness. The author reminds us that divine qualities exist inside of ourselves. She concludes with a simple meditation method taught by Sant Rajinder Singh called Jyoti Meditation, in which Sharan invites us to access our own qualities of divine light, truth, and love. As she writes in "Star Girl," when "the soul can be seen for what it truly is, each spirit shines with a wonderful brilliance. When the truth is known — everybody is a star."

— Kathryn Kruger, Ph.D.

Foreword

All Creation Sings is inspired by the spirit of Native American myth, faery lore, and eclectic mysticism to bring alive the values of love, courage, patience, perseverance, responsibility, self-discipline, compassion, humility, faith, honesty, gratitude, forgiveness and nonviolence. These values are shown as the basis of love-in-action.

With a life of love, we can find a place of peace and joy within ourselves. We see in these stories the kind of thoughts, words and deeds which could help to bring peace to families, friends, communities, and nations.

The stories also show us struggle and sorrow. We feel the pain of death, grief, loneliness, poverty, and cultural conflict, but we are not trapped in this pain, because we see how to transcend it through love.

In order to live in a world in which every single soul is respected, loved and cared for, we must learn to live that way ourselves. Only when young and old alike begin to find the reality of the love of the universe within themselves will they be able to say, as those who return from states of deep prayer and meditation say, "I felt more peace, bliss and love than I ever imagined possible. I learned that love and giving love are the most important things on earth and the reason why we all are here."

These stories speak of a world in which young and old alike are learning and living this vision.

If we are children, we can learn to live with love

now and gain ourselves peace and joy for the rest of our lives. If we are older, the inner child within us can read these stories, rejoice, heal, and live anew.

"As we think, so we become." Let us read, think and dream of a world that will reflect the heaven on earth we all wish for.

— Sharan Shively

Myth & Mystery

Mystical Stories

Death, the Maiden and Mikhail

The sun was starting to fall behind the trees as Mikhail rode at break-neck speed down the northern road to the castle. "What could be so important that my master must summon me to come 'quickest at all costs'?" thought Mikhail. The sound of his horse's galloping hooves was almost deafening. Clots of sticky mud splattered up from the heavily rutted dirt roadway.

It was late autumn. The pale slanting sunlight shone through the leaves on the trees lining the old road. Each leaf glowed like stained glass, brilliant yellow, yellow-orange or scarlet. The tree trunks and branches, dark from the rain that had fallen earlier, formed arches and arabesques framing the stained glass colors against the sky.

Suddenly a pale form darted out from the trees and stood, arms outstretched, bidding the rider halt. "It's a lass," Mikhail thought. "I must stop. She must be in danger or in need of aid."

Mikhail reined in his huge mountain-bred horse and dismounted. A slim girl, huddled in a long cloak of pale wool, stood before him.

"Kind sir," she spoke. "My name is Glynnis and I cry you mercy. I work for Lord Dyen — the Lord of Death. I have served him well for almost one full year but I must run now. I would go to the castle if I can to beg help — I've heard that Lord Toluval, the lord of the castle, is both wise and kind."

Off in the distance some creature howled. The sound echoed through the low hills. A strong wind whipped the trees from side to side sending birds flying and leaves falling to the ground.

"Lord Dyen left just this afternoon to claim my father, mother and brother," said Glynnis shakily as tears fell from eyes as sky-blue as the silk edging her cloak. "He is taking the only ones in this world that I love," she sobbed.

"Take my hand and climb up behind me, Glynnis," said Mikhail. "We will ride like the wind and reach the castle before dawn. I am going there myself. Lord Toluval is a master of ancient wisdom. I study with him. He is all-knowing and the heart of kindness itself. He will help, I know it."

They rode with God-speed as night fell. The moon and stars shone like jewels in the dark sky. It was well past midnight when they reached the castle gate. Both of them were weary, their cloaks soaked and heavy with mud.

"Who goes there?" cried the sentry.

"Mikhail and the maiden, Glynnis," replied

Mikhail. "I was summoned in all haste by Lord Toluval. Glynnis also must speak with him."

"Well-met. Ye may ride through," said the sentry, raising the iron-bound gate so they might enter.

Mikhail rode his horse to the stable and there dismounted, helping Glynnis down. He left his horse with a groom to be cared for. Then the two of them walked wearily up to the great house.

At the entranceway to the great house, Mikhail gave their names to the guards and they were told to enter. Their cloaks were taken and, after they had removed their wet and dirty boots, they were shown to an anteroom to wait while a house servant took word of their arrival to Lord Toluval.

Soon the servant returned and led them to Lord Toluval's study, high up in the highest tower of the castle. They were given cups of hot, spicy tea with generous amounts of milk and sugar. They sipped the delicious, fragrant tea while they waited for the master's arrival.

Lord Toluval's study was round. Tall window turrets were spaced evenly around its one circular wall. A cushioned window seat circled the room beneath the windows. In the center of the room, a huge desk stood. Bookcases were built into three sides of the desk. Their shelves contained volumes of all sizes — some old-looking, others new.

After some time the inner door of the study

opened and Lord Toluval approached. He was strongly built with strikingly handsome features. His hair and beard were snow white. His face, weathered with his years, radiated wisdom and kindness. He went to Mikhail and hugged him. "And who is this?" he asked, looking at the maiden.

"This is Glynnis, sir," replied Mikhail. "She serves Lord Dyen but seeks your help in desperate need. And I must know what was so important that you summoned me to come in so much haste."

"First let me hear your story, my daughter," said Lord Toluval sympathetically, offering Glynnis a chair, then taking his own seat.

"Kind sir," Glynnis started. "My parents were old when my brother, Jameth, came along. They could not keep up with our farm well enough to provide for us all. They contracted me for the time of five years to work for Lord Dyen who agreed to provide all that was necessary for them during that time and a generous dowry for me so I might marry well after the five years ended. By that time Jameth also would be old enough to find work.

"Lord Dyen has been a proper employer. I have no quarrel with that. But as I cleaned and tidied his study yesterday I saw written on a parchment a list of people to be taken away. It included the names of my mother, father and brother. They are all I love in this world and I cannot abide their dying nor can I serve the one who takes them. But I am helpless, bound by law to be Lord Dyen's servant. Nor is there anything I can do to help my family. I am helpless, helpless..." she sobbed.

As he listened, Lord Toluval's expression saddened. Compassion filled his eyes. "My child," said Lord Toluval in a soothing voice, "I know this must be hard for you, but death comes to everyone in their time. This is a law of God and nature. Everyone on earth is bound by that law. What would you have me do?"

"I cannot bear to lose them," sobbed Glynnis. "I have not seen them for a year since I left to go to Lord Dyen. I was going to visit next week when the first year of my service was done. I cannot bear to lose them and it's even worse because I didn't even have a chance to say good-bye." Glynnis shuddered and wept deep, racking sobs of complete anguish.

"Can you not help her somehow?" pleaded Mikhail.

"Let us go into the overworld. It is God absolute who has created and rules all. Lord Dyen — death — is a servant of the absolute Lord. We will call him. Perhaps he will be kind enough to explain why he chooses to take Glynnis's family now," said Lord Toluval. He closed his eyes and became utterly still. The lights inside the room began to glow brighter. The air shimmered and a deep vibration could be heard.

He opened his eyes. "We are in the overworld," he said, "and I have asked Lord Dyen to meet us here."

Mikhail looked around. He saw a sunny glade lined with fruit-laden trees. Blossoming flowers grew everywhere, and their fragrance perfumed the air. All of the colors were glowing as if lit by an inner light.

Glynnis no longer wore her plain wool gown. Here, she wore a shimmering, silken gown of pastel colors that rippled like water forming and reforming lovely patterns. Mikhail wore a tunic and trousers in the same shifting patterns but in deeper, more vibrant colors. Lord Toluval wore garments so shining-white that they cast light all around. Then Glynnis saw Lord Dyen. He was dressed in deep black that absorbed the light around him. He came near.

"Lord Toluval, young sir, Glynnis," Lord Dyen greeted them courteously.

"Respected sir," said Lord Toluval to Lord Dyen. "Glynnis has told us that your plan was to take her parents and brother into your domain today. She feels that this is less than she deserves from you as your loyal servant. I wonder if you would care to tell us anything about your decision."

"Dear Glynnis, I knew that this would pain you," said Lord Dyen. "But I had to choose from among several possible fates that the supreme Creator, God, had laid down. The village that your parents live in will be overtaken by bandits next week. The old people will be killed cruelly or wounded and left untended to die in sorrow. The young people will be captured and taken into lives of the harshest sort of slavery. This was set in motion hundreds of lifetimes ago by actions performed by the souls who live now as these villagers. You were due to visit your parents next week so you and your brother would have been captured and sold into slavery as your parents lay dying.

"As Lord of the Domain of Death I have some discretionary powers. I chose to take your parents and brother quickly and easily now so that they and you would be spared the horrible pain that might have been...."

Glynnis looked stunned. It was clear that she was trying to understand what Lord Dyen had said.

"What has become of her family? Where have you taken them?" asked Lord Toluval.

Lord Dyen gestured with his hand and a frame appeared in the sky. There was a large painting within the frame, but the painting seemed to be alive. On it could be seen a country village nestled in a shady dell. As Glynnis and the others looked, they saw more closely and were able to look through the stone walls of one of the cottages. There Glynnis saw three people sitting comfortably before a cozy fire.

"It's Ma and Pa and Jameth!" exclaimed Glynnis. "They look so healthy, so glowing, so happy!"

"Death is not the bitter evil many think it is, Glynnis," said Lord Dyen.

"Life is a series of plays that the Creator, God, scripts for us," said Lord Toluval. "Our souls never die. We go from play to play as our Creator wills. Death is only a change from one place, one script, to another. In each play our souls learn wisdom so that finally, one day, we will learn how to come to our true Home and conscious union with God. Until then we must have faith that what He gives us is truly for our highest good."

"I am ashamed, sir," said Glynnis to Lord Dyen.

"No, no, Glynnis. All is well," he replied. "I hope to see you when your vacation is over. Sir..." he looked at Lord Toluval. "May I take leave of you?"

Lord Toluval nodded graciously, "Go with God," he said. Lord Dyen disappeared.

"Sir!" said Mikhail eagerly. "What was it that caused you to summon me with such haste?"

Lord Toluval smiled at Mikhail and even more tenderly at Glynnis. "Let us return to earth now, and then I will tell you." He closed his eyes. Again the air shimmered and the deep vibration sounded. When he opened his eyes, all three of them were once again in Lord Toluval's study.

"Sir?" asked Mikhail.

"Patience, young lad," laughed Lord Toluval.

He looked at Glynnis kindly. "I know that even with your new understanding, the deaths of your only loved ones will still cause you heartbreak and sorrow," he said to her. "May I ask you to consider me as your father? I would love you as the daughter I have never had and cherish, protect and nurture you."

"Oh, dear Lord Toluval," cried Glynnis. "I accept with all my heart. I shall grieve for my family but my grief will be so comforted by the warmth and sweetness of your loving kindness."

"Ahem," Mikhail cleared his throat and tapped his foot upon the floor.

"In a moment, Mikhail. I must speak with Glynnis first," said Lord Toluval.

"I would like you to learn to meditate so you will find the inner peace that will comfort you most, Glynnis," Lord Toluval said, smiling. "Please sit as comfortably as you can," he said, pointing to a cozy armchair in a little alcove. "Close your eyes and look sweetly into the darkness you see in front of you with your inner eyes. Repeat any name of God you love with the speech of your thoughts," he told her, as he gently pressed his thumb between her two eyebrows. She smiled softly and her face eased as she went into a deep trance.

When Lord Toluval returned from putting

Glynnis into meditation, he went to the tower window which looked down upon the castle keep and the northern road and rolling hills beyond it. "Mikhail, have you been betrothed yet?" he asked.

"No, sir," replied Mikhail. "My parents have not yet settled on anyone suitable. They say I am too adventurous. I am too full of dreams and imaginings for most girls, they say."

"I asked you to ride with all haste, Mikhail," said Lord Toluval, "because I knew that only if you hurried would you be in time to meet Glynnis as she stood upon the northern road. In four years she will be able to pick and choose among suitors, I imagine. But you and she have shared a special vision together. Perhaps, if it is agreeable to you, you may visit her from time to time. If all goes well, your friendship will grow and four years hence, if my guess is right, you may choose each other as life partners. If I am right, you and she will have a wonderful basis for a happy life together."

Lord Toluval looked affectionately at Mikhail. "Say nothing of this to Glynnis, boy," he said. "She has suffered a grievous loss. I will look out for her, and meditation and time will help her through it. Still, you must go slowly as you seek her friendship."

Mikhail looked both stunned and grateful. He said "I will follow your advice, sir, and I thank you for it, and for the wisdom and love that lies behind it."

Through the tower window, Mikhail could see that the dark sky, glittering with stars, had started to brighten towards the east as the sun began to rise. Time rode on, faster than the wind, but slow enough for love to grow in the kingdom of day and night. 🦢

The Gift of All Names

A long time ago a fearful dragon terrorized the entire kingdom from the deep Blue Ocean to the great Gray Mountain. This dragon appeared one day in the sky two weeks before the new year. All of a sudden he was there. Then, he was breathing a huge, surging torrent of flame down onto a ripe corn field, burning it beyond all recognition.

After burning the field, the dragon landed. He spoke in the language of the kingdom. His voice was as loud and deep as a bass drum, "Unless you give me two treasure chests of gold and jewels I will burn every field of grain in this entire land to the ground. You have two weeks. I will wait at the largest cave at the foot of the Gray Mountain. Bring the treasure there or regret it!"

The farmers went to the king. The king told his ministers to take two treasure chests of gold and jewels from the treasury to the Gray Mountain and leave them at the dragon's lair.

Each year after that the dragon appeared two weeks before the new year and repeated his message.

Nobody wanted to fight with the dragon, so each year the king sent the treasure as demanded.

One year the king's ministers went to the dragon's cave four weeks before the new year. The chief minister saw a large gong and hammer hanging from a wooden frame next to the opening of the cave. The minister struck the gong as hard as he could with the hammer. After the reverberations faded away, the dragon appeared at the mouth of the cave. "What would you with me?" the dragon asked.

"If we give you two full treasure chests each year," the minister said, "in seven years our treasury will be empty. Is there any other tribute you will accept?"

"Yes," the dragon roared. "Tell me my true name and I will take that as final tribute and leave your kingdom in peace," he said. "But if you do not tell me my true name, or you do not bring the treasure, then I shall burn every one of your fields to the ground!"

The king called a meeting of everyone in the kingdom from his ministers to his pages and all of his citizens, including the little children. "This problem is so dire it concerns everybody," he said. He asked them all to try to find ways to deal with the dragon. "Consult any wise woman or man you may know of, my children," he said, "for we are in desperate need."

That year the king sent scientists to the dragon. They named all the biological categories of snake, lizard and dinosaur, hoping that among these kindred would be the dragon's name.

"No!" roared the dragon. So two treasure chests of tribute had to be paid.

Next year the philosophers tried. They postulated as their first axiom that the dragon flew in the sky. They then proposed the following theorem: All birds fly; the dragon flies; therefore the dragon is a bird. They went to the dragon and read out all the names of every species of bird in existence....

"No!" roared the dragon. That year also two treasure chests of tribute were paid.

Next year all the poets gathered. They wrote an epic about the heroic exploits of a dragon. They rhymed with the word dragon as much as possible. They hoped that among those rhymes would be his true name. They went to the dragon and dramatically recited the great epic. Alas — as the echoes faded, the dragon roared "No!"

That year also two treasure chests of tribute had to be paid.

The next year all the merchants computed the dragon's approximate shipping weight, market value and value as trade goods. They read out their final sum in every known currency of the world to the dragon.

Nobody was much surprised when the dragon roared "No!"

Then all the artists painted a great triptych. The

paintings represented the youth, adulthood and old age of a dragon. It was acknowledged by all as the greatest work of art ever accomplished within the kingdom or, in fact, the known world. The paintings were carefully wrapped and transported to the dragon's cave where they were carefully assembled and presented. The entire kingdom held its breath....

"No!" roared the dragon, carefully avoiding hitting the paintings with his tail as he stumped back into his lair. That year also the tribute was paid.

The next year all the musicians and dancers of the kingdom composed and choreographed a ballet — The Dance of the Dragon. It was the greatest work of its type ever created. It was performed by the best musicians and dancers of the world. The kingdom and the world at large wept when the dragon roared "No!" That year, also, the tribute was paid.

It was now the seventh year. After the failure of The Dance of the Dragon, when the tribute was paid, the treasurer of the kingdom had announced the kingdom's bankruptcy.

Meanwhile, a boy named Sunny had just turned fourteen. He had seen his older brothers and sisters questioning the wise men and women of their neighborhood, but all to no avail. He saw that nobody had any idea what to do. He decided he would not sit idly by as the dragon burned to cinders every field in the kingdom, his family's among them. He knew that everyone in the entire kingdom had tried their hardest to guess the dragon's true name but he had not yet tried.

A large number of books from all over the world had been collected and stored in the university of the capital city of the kingdom. Sunny knew that the library of the university (where all the books were kept) would have all the knowledge known to humankind within its doors. Since the farmer's market where his family sold the fruits and vegetables they raised was located near the university, he asked his father if he could go with him the next time his father went to the city.

The next week Sunny traveled to the capital with his father. Once there he walked to the university library, went in and asked for the head librarian. Her name was Saraswati. She agreed to help Sunny in his search for the dragon's true name. They looked up the word dragon in every language recorded in the library and Sunny carefully wrote all the names down.

When he and his father got home from the city, Sunny asked his mother and father for permission to travel to the Gray Mountain to see the dragon. His parents didn't want him to go alone. They felt the journey was too dangerous for a young boy, but they had to stay behind to tend their garden and fields.

"Father, Mother," Sunny said. "The dragon has

never harmed a human being in all the years he has been here. This is the year our kingdom will not be able to pay the tribute. Since we will have no gold or jewels to pay the dragon, someone must guess his true name or he will destroy all the grain fields of the kingdom and ours will be among them. I know all of the scientists, philosophers and artists have failed, but perhaps — if it is the will of God — I may succeed."

Reluctantly, his parents agreed to let him go. Next morning, bright and early, Sunny set out. He took a pack with provisions and his list of names and walked towards the Gray Mountain. At last, he reached there as the sun was setting. He took the huge hammer resting by the brass gong and beat upon it.

The dragon appeared at the mouth of his cave. "What would you with me, boy?" he boomed.

"Sir Dragon," said Sunny respectfully. " My name is Sunny and I have a list of dragon names from every recorded language in the great library of our capital city. I would like to read them to you, if I may, for perhaps your true name is among them."

"You may read them, boy," said the dragon speaking as gently as he could.

Sunny unrolled his parchment and read out the following names:

A'las (Bicol)

Bitin (Cebuano)

Drak (Czech)

Dragon (English)

Dragon (French)

Drachen (German)

Feethee (Greek)

Kuchar (Haryanvi)

Nakra (Hindi)

Sarkany (Hungarian)

Dragon (Italian)

Wasz (Polish)

Drakon (Russian)

Detya (Sanskrit)

Drak (Slovakian)

Dragon (Spanish)

Dambuhala (Tagalog)

Asur (Telegu)

Sasabonsam (Twi)

Sunny looked at the dragon hopefully. "Well?" he asked.

"I'm sorry, boy," said the dragon sadly. "You have not found my true name. But it is night now and dark and cold here in the mountains. Please stay inside the cave a little distance for the night. The warmth of my fire will keep you cozy and you will be sheltered and warm. Start back for your home tomorrow when the sun shines."

Sunny was surprised at the dragon's kindness. It seemed strange that such a fierce beast would speak in such a gentle and caring way. Still, the puzzle of the dragon's kindness could only be added to the greater puzzle of how to find his true name. Sunny's parents had taught him that courtesy was the correct response at all times so he politely replied, "I will, Sir Dragon, and may God bless you for your kindness."

The next morning Sunny left the cave where he had sheltered and set out for home. He reached there at sunset. He told his mother and father of his failure. They looked worried and sad to hear it.

Then his mother said, "Do not unpack your travel bag, Sunny. My own father's father is a very ancient and wise man. He prefers to live alone and spend his days in meditation, but our trouble now is seemingly beyond hope. I think we must consult him. Tomorrow go to the forest and take the path through the berry bog. After you have passed through the bog, you will see a large hill. At the bottom of the hill, a boulder hides a cave. Within that cave, my revered grandfather abides. Seek him there. Perhaps he will have the answer we need."

So the next day Sunny took his pack and provisions and set out for the forest. He crossed over the berry bog path as the sun was standing straight up in the heavens and had a bit of noon-time food before starting to look for the cave of the ancient wise man. As he was just finishing his bread and cheese, for such was his noon-time meal, he saw an old, old man walking towards him.

Sunny rose to his feet and folded his hands in respect to the ancient one. "Kind sir, are you the wise man of the forest?" he asked. "If so, you are the grandfather of my respected mother."

The old man smiled "Yes, I am your great-grandfather, but I am just a man like any other. If you call me wise, I will tell you that long ago I learned that wisdom comes from harmony with God, not 'whys'."

"But sir, can you help me?" asked Sunny.

"If you will tell me what you need I will see whether I can help or not," the old man replied.

"There is a dragon that threatens our kingdom. I must learn his true name," Sunny said, breathlessly. "If I cannot, he will destroy every field of grain in the kingdom and we will all fall into starvation and ruin."

"With the grace of God I can tell you what must be done and, if you can do as I tell you, you may receive the help you need."

"Oh, sir. Please tell me. I will do exactly as you say," said Sunny, gratefully.

The old man closed his eyes a moment and then, opening them, he spoke. "You must sit comfortably anywhere here that you can sit still for the longest time. Then you must close your eyes and repeat with the tongue of your thought whatever name of God is dearest to you. As you mentally repeat this name, you must look with your inner eye, the eye of your soul, into the darkness you see in front of you. As you continue to look, the Light of God will appear to you and, as you gaze into it, the true name of the dragon will become known to you."

Sunny sat upon the soft moss and fallen leaves of the forest floor. He closed his eyes and did as the ancient one had instructed.

Some time later he opened his eyes, jumped up and ran to the ancient one who sat nearby resting against a gnarled tree trunk.

"Well, Sunny," queried the ancient one. "Do you know the dragon's true name?"

"Oh, sir," said Sunny. "I do!"

"Then go, boy," said the ancient one. "Go to the dragon's lair in the Gray Mountain and I will go tell your parents not to worry."

Sunny went with the speed of youth and joy. Again he took the large hammer and struck the brass gong at the mouth of the cave. Again the dragon appeared.

"Well, boy?" the dragon asked.

"Sir Dragon, I believe I know your true name," Sunny said.

"Speak, boy," replied the dragon.

Sunny ran over to the huge dragon and placed a sweet kiss upon his forepaw. "My brother," he said, "your true name is Soul for you are a child of God as are we all."

"Yes!" roared the dragon.

Then, to Sunny's amazement, the dragon's scaly hide started to split. Deep rents appeared, widened and ran together. All of a sudden, with an explosive hiss the dragon's hide fell away and a handsome young man in regal attire stood revealed.

"Sunny," said this young man, "I was bespelled one hundred years ago by an evil magician and forced to live as a dragon. The spell could only be broken if someone discovered my true name. How came you by this knowledge?"

"I repeated the name of God until His Light took my soul up into the regions of all Love. It was there I discovered that all souls in creation are brothers and sisters in God and there is only one language — the language of the heart. This language gives us the gift of all names as all are One in the Lord."

"Come Sunny, brother," said the boy who had been a dragon. "Let us go to celebrate our freedom."

And it came to pass that the young man, a prince from another land, returned the treasures and jewels to the treasury and helped to plant new seeds in the fields he had formerly ruined. Having done so, he returned to his homeland which he had left so long ago.

As for Sunny, when asked what he wanted as a reward for saving the kingdom, he asked the king and queen for permission to marry the royal princess. The king and queen gladly granted his wish, and the engagement of Sunny and the princess was announced at a gala royal ball.

Sunny graduated from his local high school and then attended the university where the great library was. After graduating from the university, Sunny and the princess were married. Invitations to the wedding were sent to everyone in the entire kingdom. The wedding was held outdoors so that there would be room for all the people who wished to attend. It was the most beautiful wedding ever held. Sunny's best man was the prince who had been a dragon, and the wedding ring was a gift from the former dragon's own treasure chests — a golden band covered with diamonds, emeralds, rubies and sapphires.

After the wedding festivities were over, the king requested Sunny to work as his top minister. Sunny had become a very learned man, but whenever worldly knowledge failed, he sat in meditation which gave him access to the highest wisdom.

William and the Wood Wraith

Will ran out to the apple tree in their back yard, picked up a windfall from the ground, checked it for worms and, finding none, bit into it. It was a winesap apple, tart-sweet and juicy. He was on his way to the old treehouse he and his dad had built three summers ago in the big maple that stood at the outside edge of their property.

When he got there he climbed up the makeshift ladder, crawled through the low door opening and inside. It was dusty and some fallen leaves and bits of branches had blown in, but it was great to be there. He threw out the bigger debris. Then, taking a rag he kept tucked in the corner, he got out the worst of the dust. Sitting down, he opened the tin box that held his old comic books. He was just starting to read when all of a sudden the autumn sunshine outside the rough-screened window openings flared up so brightly it made Will's eyes hurt. Then, it dimmed so he could hardly see.

A strange keening wind that sounded like a ghost movie wailed around the tree house which shuddered and shifted as the branches it was fastened to blew back and forth.

Will put the comic he was reading carefully back in the tin box. Then, he tried to leave, but found he couldn't get through the door opening. It looked open but some kind of force field or something kept pushing him back!

As he looked, horrified, a thin, pale, twisted hand materialized out of the air at the doorway and shoved him hard. He fell back, sprawling, onto the floor. A strange creature was forming itself starting at that hideous hand. The creature was pale and looked misty like fog. It was about six feet tall, sort of human-shaped, with a head, a face, a trunk like a tree and weird-looking arms and legs that were gnarled and twisted like branches.

"I am a wood wraith," the creature said in a voice that was a softer version of the wind still howling outside the tree house. "The spirit of the earth, our mother, has sent me."

"What do you want with me?" asked Will bravely.

"You humans killed me, my family and all my forest with your deadly rain of poison," the wood wraith said.

"You mean acid rain?" asked Will.

"We stood exposed to the rain of pain, torture and death condemned by your uncaring, unthinking race to die long, horrible deaths," the wraith said.

"I'm really sorry," said Will. "But I'm just a kid. I didn't do it and I couldn't help it."

"You, as well as others, have been chosen," the wraith said menacingly.

"Chosen for what?" asked Will, his voice quivering just a little.

"You will see," the wraith replied. He touched Will on the shoulder. His pale, mist-like, knobby hand was cold and dripping something slimy and wet. Will shuddered.

Everything got dark. The tree house was gone and Will and the wood wraith stood upon a rocky ledge at the top of a high mountain. As Will looked he could see two different scenes in front of him. It was as if the view had been evenly split into two halves. It was like two different worlds side by side.

Everything looked miniature like a toy landscape for a model train or the view from an airplane window as it got far up above the ground. As Will looked, he saw that one world was green with miniature houses and fields and lakes and trees and one was all water. There were no buildings, no animals, and no people. There was nothing at all except water.

"Why am I here? What am I seeing?" asked Will.

"You're seeing the two futures possible for your world," replied the wood wraith.

Will looked as carefully as he could. It was as if

his intention to look very intently magnified his ability to see, and the two different views came into closer focus like looking through binoculars.

In one world there was only water — nothing else — stretching endlessly in every direction as far as he could see. The other world looked more like his own home. There were towns, roads, homes, lawns, fields, trees, streams, lakes and people. He thought he saw horses and cows. Everything looked strong, well-cared-for, and healthy.

"But why am I seeing this?" he asked. "If I have been chosen, who has chosen me and what for? Won't someone tell me? Please?" Will asked.

The wind that had been wailing all this time suddenly ceased. A gentle, warm breeze that smelled of apple blossoms ruffled Will's hair. He turned around. A motherly woman dressed in many shades of green stood there. She wore a garland of trilliums and violets. Her hair was brown like tree bark. Her eyes were the blue of delphiniums. She smiled. It was like sunshine streaming out from behind clouds on a rainy day. "I am Mother Gaia," she said.

"What am I doing here?" asked Will. "What is this about?"

"I am the spirit of the earth," Mother Gaia replied. "Human beings are at a crossroads. Some things are predestined, but some things depend on free will. All living things and nature should live together in harmony. If human beings destroy this harmony, our lands, fresh water, forests, air and life itself, as we know it, may be destroyed. Already the destruction of so many forests and air pollution has caused global warming. The polar ice caps are melting. The oceans are rising. If humanity can't live in harmony with other creatures and the earth itself, the future will be bleak indeed. But it's not too late. Each person can still choose to help. Everyone must choose for himself or herself. Think carefully, Will, but think with your heart."

The wood wraith touched Will's shoulder. Again the scene around them dimmed. When Will's vision cleared he stood in a forest glade. He saw ghostly apparitions in a long line moving towards him. As they came closer he saw they were many kinds of birds and animals as well as people of all ages and races. They all looked sickly, undernourished, weak, malformed and deformed. "I can hardly stand it," he thought. "I can't bear to see them so miserable."

As they moved past him, a tiger with her cub, gaunt and hardly able to walk, looked sadly at him. A Golden monkey, carrying her dying and deformed young one limply in her arms, looked at him imploringly. People of all ages and colors, wearing different kinds of clothing, but all weak, sick and barely moving, turned huge, pleading eyes towards him. Each spoke words he could understand all too well, "Help us. Please, please help us."

Will's heart was heavy with sorrow and shame. "Has humanity harmed ecology so badly that all this pain and destruction must occur?" he shouted. "I won't let it. I will help. I will learn how to help!"

The line of tortured apparitions disappeared. Mother Gaia was there instead. "I want to help, Mother Gaia," said Will. "But why have you chosen me to see this? I'm still young, and I can't do anything by myself."

Mother Gaia waved her hand. Will saw what appeared to be thousands of glowing movie screens superimposed against the background of the forest's trees. In each of the screens a boy or girl close to Will's age but of a different nationality or culture was standing next to a being that looked like the wood wraith and talking to Mother Gaia. "Young people are not bound by the mistakes of the past, Will," she said. "You and others like you are the hope of the future."

She looked sweetly into Will's eyes. "Nobody can change anybody else, but each person can change herself or himself. If you want to understand, you will. If you want to help, you will find ways. If you help, others will be affected by you and the good ways will grow. And you won't be alone for long. Some day your brothers and sisters from all over the world will find you."

"What can I do to start?" Will asked.

"First — love," said Mother Gaia. "Love is most important because all good thoughts, words and deeds come naturally from a loving heart.

"Second — take only what you need.

"Third — give back as much as you can. It's not fabulous wealth that fills our hearts with joy; it's living the right way. When you take only what you really need and give back as much as you can in as many ways as you can, you feel happy naturally.

"Fourth, though really the same as the first — take time to discover your own divine nature by meditating on the Light of God within you. As you do, your heart will naturally become loving."

Mother Gaia smiled and raised her hand. Sparkling sunlight flowed in strong beams from her fingers. The light touched Will and the wood wraith. Will felt a wonderful, cheerful, joyous energy throughout him. The wood wraith lost his misty gray, tortured appearance and became round and smooth. The bark on his trunk became a healthy dark brown and his hair looked like dark green evergreen needles. The fragrance of sweet balsam filled the air.

A gentle, clean, clear rain fell in the forest glade. Where it touched the sunlight radiating from Mother Gaia, sparkling rainbows appeared. Flowers sprouted from the forest floor and blossomed. Birds flew in the sky twittering in a joyful chorus. Animals of all kinds and sizes ran and played with their young ones and each other.

"Balance and harmony between humanity, earth and nature will bring peace and happiness for all," Mother Gaia said.

"I believe you, Mother," said Will. "And I'll keep that belief always in my heart."

"We must go now," said the wood wraith who was wretched and wraith-like no longer. He touched Will on the shoulder. His touch was warm and gentle. Everything grew dim and when Will could see again, he saw the walls of the tree house around him. He quickly went out, climbed down and ran toward home. As he passed the apple tree he stopped to give it a friendly pat. "I never appreciated you enough," he said to it. "But I sure will now." A world of new possibilities awaited him. He ran towards that world joyfully.

Cinderallie

nce, in a country far in distance but near in heart, there lived a girl who wished for wonder. Her name was Allie and she longed for beauty and enchantment, magic and mystery.

One day word was sent out far and wide announcing that the king and queen wished to arrange the marriage of their son, the prince. In order to do this, the king and queen would hold a tea party and a grand ball. Every girl of sixteen to twenty years was invited to the tea party wherein they would all meet the prince and have a chance to chat with him. Then, in the evening, the girls would attend a ball where the prince would choose the girl he liked the most. The king and queen would meet his chosen one and, if they agreed with his choice, the prince and the lucky girl would be engaged.

All of the countryside was in a state of excitement. Everywhere, girls rushed about deciding on hairdos and clothing, shoes and jewelry. Everywhere they practiced dancing and curtsying, chatting and conversing.

What did Allie do? She watched her sisters Tonia and Sonia trying on clothes and practicing dancing. They were so tall and graceful, so clever and so charming. Allie was in awe of them. How could she belong to the same family? She was small and chubby and clumsy. In her heart, Allie dreamed of going to the tea party and the ball, but in her mind she felt there was little hope. Oh she could do some things — she could heal a robin's broken wing and nurse an ailing plant back to life. She could ease her mom's headaches and her dad's worries. But could she dance? No. And could she chat? No. And could she look beautiful? Maybe...

But there were four weeks until the tea party and the ball. In that four weeks she would try to learn what she had to. So the next day she set out for dancing class. But on the way, she saw the kitten who lived next door stuck way up in the highest branches of a tall tree. It had climbed up but didn't know how to get down and it was meowing and yowling with fear.

"Don't worry, kitty, kitty," said Allie, "I'll help you." And she ran home to get help. But nobody was home. "If I take the ladder and help the kitty myself, I'll miss dancing class. If I don't learn to dance I won't have a chance with the prince. But the kitty's so scared. I can't bear to leave it that way. What if nobody else helps it get down? I have to do it. I'll do it just as fast as I can." So she took the ladder, climbed up, coaxed the kitten into her arms and then climbed down. As she took the kitten home, she saw the sun was setting. Dancing class was over.

That night Allie asked her mom to practice chatting, but mom's head hurt so Allie gave her a neck rub. By the time she was finished, it was time for bed.

Oh well, there was still some time left. She'd learn what she had to before it was too late. She was sure of it.

But each afternoon something else happened. Mrs. Jentry who was old and lived alone in a house down the street got sick and needed help every day for a whole week. "I'm missing dancing class," Allie thought. "And I haven't found a dress yet either, but I love Mrs. Jentry and she has nobody else to help her. I want her to get better. I have to do it."

Somehow, the weeks raced by. There had been a drought and no rain had fallen. Mom and dad both worked. Tonia and Sonia were practicing and sewing. Only Allie had time to water the garden. But it took so much time. She had to carry bucket after bucket from their well. "If I don't do it the plants will wither and die," she thought, and she loved them, so she did it.

If it wasn't one thing it was another. Allie was busy every day. She asked her sisters for help at night, but they wouldn't practice dancing with her — she knew nothing, they said — it was hopeless. They wouldn't practice chatting either, because there, too, her skills were so far beneath theirs, they might lose their edge if they practiced with her. "And it's so close, now," they said, "it's only a week away."

Then, the family milk cow hurt her leg on a broken board. Each night Allie went to her, cleaned her cut and put salve and a fresh bandage on the sore spot. She asked Tonia and Sonia if they would take turns helping. "Oh, you're more suited to dealing with a smelly old cow, dear," they smirked. Allie hadn't done anything she needed to for the ball, but how could she leave old Bessie uncared for?

So now half a week was left. That night, Allie's mom called her over. "Do you want to go to the ball, Allie?" she asked.

"Well, I guess so, Mom. But I don't know..." and her voice trailed off.

"But why wouldn't you go, dear? Everyone's invited."

"Well," said Allie, "I have nothing to wear and I can't curtsy, chat or dance, and it's only a few days away."

"Oh don't worry," said her mom. "I'll teach you all you need to know in no time at all."

She quickly showed Allie how to curtsy. They practiced some easy chatting phrases, and then, holding hands, the two of them whirled around the room in a simple waltz.

"That's wonderful," said Allie. "Maybe it isn't perfect, but it's enough for me to give it a good, solid try. But, Mom, what can I wear?"

"I have a dress," said her mom. "I wore it years ago for my graduation day. That will do for the tea. As for the ball? I've been working an extra hour each day since the ball was announced. You've helped me so much. Your loving care has washed my pains away. The extra money I earned is for you. Take it and buy a gown, shoes, and jewelry."

Allie's heart overflowed. She hugged her mom and ran up to bed where her heart danced with her dreams all night.

But, somehow, things kept on happening. It still hadn't rained and watering the garden took hours. Mrs. Jentry was a lot better, but she still needed someone to look in on her. Dad sat on his reading glasses and someone had to help him with his paperwork at night. Mom couldn't do it because close work brought on her headaches, so Allie did. All of a sudden it was Saturday, the day of the tea party and the ball.

Tonia and Sonia were dressed to perfection. They called a cab and left for the afternoon tea. "You'd better hurry, Allie," they called as they drove away.

"But I haven't bought my ball gown yet," thought Allie as she hurried down the street to the store.

When she got there, she ran to Periwinkle's. It

was the oldest and best shop in town. As she got there, she started to rush in but wait — who was that, looking sadly at the gowns displayed in the shop window? Why it was Megan and she was crying. Everyone knew Megan's family was very poor — probably she couldn't afford to buy a dress for the ball.

"Don't worry, Megan," said Allie, "I have a lot of money. I'm sure it's enough for both of us." And, taking Megan by the hand, Allie led her gaily into Periwinkle's.

"Ma'am," said Allie to the saleswoman, "Please find a ball gown for Megan here. And then one for me."

So Megan found a beautiful gown. Allie paid for it and Megan ran home to change for the tea party while Allie tried on gowns. She found the perfect one, but when she went to pay for it, she found she didn't have enough money. When the saleswoman showed her the rack of gowns she could afford, Allie felt sick. All she could afford was plain, unbleached muslin — no silk, no pretty colors, no sequins, and no jewels or accessories either. But it was all she could do now, so she bought one and left.

By now it was really late. She ran all the way home. By the time she reached there, however, it was so late the tea party was already over.

"Oh, well," she thought, "I've missed the tea party, but I did the best I could. I won't give up! I'm going to get dressed and go to the ball." So she ran upstairs, washed, brushed her hair, put on her plain muslin gown and her best shoes and went to the ball.

Meanwhile, the prince, the king and the queen had met and chatted with all the eligible girls of the country, including Sonia, Tonia and Megan, who had arrived late. Now the girls were dressing for the ball and the king and queen were talking with Reggie, the prince.

"Well, dear?" asked the queen.

"I don't know, Mom," said Reggie.

"But there were so many lovely girls," said the queen.

"And they were so beautiful and so charming," said the king.

"But, I don't know...something was missing," said Reggie. "Maybe tonight at the ball I'll be more sure."

That night at the ball, Allie entered breathlessly and ran up to Tonia and Sonia. They stared at Allie's plain cotton gown and said, "Where did you get that?"

"At Periwinkle's," said Allie.

"Did they use it to dust the shelves?" laughed Sonia.

"My dear," smirked Tonia, "you look lovely, but that plain white cotton deadens the colors of our gowns. Would you mind terribly not standing next to us?" And smiling oh–so sweetly, Tonia took Sonia's arm and drew her away.

Then Allie ran up to Megan. To her surprise she

saw that Megan was wearing a lot of jewelry. "Hi, Megan," she said.

"Hi, Allie," said Megan.

"Where did you get the earrings, bracelets, and necklaces?" asked Allie.

"They are family heirlooms, the only things of value we own," said Megan. "My mother loaned them to me for the ball, hoping they might impress the prince."

"You have so many," said Allie. "Do you think I could borrow, maybe, just one?"

"Gee, Allie," said Megan, "I appreciate what you did for me buying me this gown and all, but you wouldn't want me to lessen my chances, would you?"

"No, of course not, Meggy," said Allie and walked away, smiling bravely.

And then, with a fanfare of trumpets, the king, queen and prince arrived.

"To start the ball, we'll have a promenade," said the king. "Will all you young ladies please pair up, walk past our dear son, Reggie, and greet him as you pass? He wants to meet each one of you."

The air hummed with excitement. The girls flew into pairs and rushed to stand in line to meet the prince. But when Allie ran up to someone to be her pair-partner, the other girl would look at her with contempt, amusement or shock, and move quickly away.

So, at the end of the line stood Allie; chubby, plainly dressed and all alone. Slowly, slowly, the line moved past the king, the queen and the prince. Every girl moved so gracefully. Every girl curtsied so beautifully. Tonia's hairdo and makeup were fabulously beautiful. Megan's jewels glittered. Sonia's gown shimmered.

But the prince, though polite and sweet to all, lingered with none. Finally, at the end of the line stood Allie. She looked at the prince's sweet and loving face and smiled. Then she curtsied — a bit stiffly, but decently, all things considered.

When the prince saw Allie, his face brightened and a broad, beaming smile appeared. "Yes," he cried. "I smell the fragrance of love and compassion. I see the beauty of unselfish caring and helping. This is the girl of my dreams."

And the king who was very wise, nodded his head.

And the queen who was also very wise, nodded her head. But then, whispering, she said to the prince, "Shouldn't you chat just a little, dear, I mean, in all fairness..."

So Reggie looked sweetly at Allie and said, " I'd like to chat with you, Allie, but I'm not good at that sort of thing. What I care about is helping the sick and needy, caring for the poor, the land and our animal friends. May I ask you something?" he said. "Tell me, dear Allie, if you were to be my wife, some day the queen of our land, would you spend your time and my money first on yourself or on caring for and helping others?"

"Well, it's strange that you should ask that, actually," replied Allie. "I would always help someone in pain or need first. I would always help the poor, the animals and the land first. In fact, dear Reggie, that is why I'm dressed so plainly today. But, truthfully?" she said, smiling shyly, "If we had enough money to help others and still had some left over, well, I like pretty things as much as the next girl." And she laughed joyfully as she did a full twirl ending with a pirouette, grand curtsy and bow.

Smiling joyfully, the prince said, "Father, Mother, this is definitely the girl I've been waiting for." And leaning closer to his father, Reggie whispered something into his ear and the king, who was not just an ordinary king, joyously lifted his hand.

Whereupon, butterflies flew from all the corners of the kingdom to give the gift of their colors to Allie's gown and then, laughing as only butterflies can, flew out into the midsummer's eve air. And flowers appeared suddenly in the air. They rained from the ceiling to touch Allie's face and lend their colors to her eyelids, cheeks and lips. Then they circled gaily around the ballroom in perfect patterns of grace leaving the perfume of their fragrances behind them before they rose up to the ceiling to hang there as garlands. Then, unbelievably, tiny miniature stars raced from the heavens above to create sparkling jewels for Allie's earrings, bracelets and necklaces and then — singing as only fallen stars, rising, can — lifted joyously back to their places in the heavens.

"May I have the pleasure of presenting to you my betrothed?" asked the prince, bowing low to all the assembly.

"Have you anything to say, dear?" asked the queen of Allie.

"Anything at all," murmured the king, realizing her shyness.

"Well, I wasn't able to practice chatting a lot, but I can recite one of my favorite verses," said Allie, and recited:

> *Kind hearts are the gardens,*
> *Kind thoughts are the roots*
> *Kind words are the flowers and*
> *Kind deeds are the fruits.*

Then, smiling shyly, she curtsied to all.

"Let the ball begin," said the prince. And he danced with Allie, a jolly, unfashionable, rollicking wonderful dance. And the king and queen danced. And everyone there danced. And the palace resounded with joyous music that touched every

heart. Except for Megan's. She had to hurry home because she was afraid her mother's jewels might fall off and get lost and she really needed them now — who knows when she'd have to impress someone next.

As for Tonia and Sonia, there was a puzzled, gloomy look on their faces for quite some time, but eventually the music cleared the gloom away and joyously they joined in and the music played on and on while a girl named Allie danced with stars in her eyes and love in her heart till dawn. 🦋

Raggedy Ann and Andy

nce there was a girl named Andrewlina. Andrewlina was a strange name for a girl, but her father had wanted a son to name Andrew. Since Andrewlina was the only child, she got the name. Her mother, realizing it was a strange name for a girl, called her Andy.

Andy's parents both worked, so they employed a housekeeper to look after the house and Andy along with it. Mrs. Brill, the housekeeper, was kind but not outgoing. She took care of the necessities, but wasn't somebody Andy wanted to spend time with. Her parents were gone all day, got home late and naturally needed the evenings to relax. So Andy couldn't really spend much time with them either.

Andy attended a private girl's school some distance away. Her parents thought she'd get a better education there. Andy was a quiet girl who didn't make friends easily, so living some distance from her school meant she had no schoolmates or neighborhood friends to play with.

She often felt terribly lonely. She spent a lot of time reading books and she talked a lot to her oldest doll, Raggedy Ann, a beaten–up rag doll she'd had for years. In fact, one day during one of their frequent tea parties in the garden, Andy confided to the raggedy old doll just how very much she longed for a real friend.

What Andy didn't know was that Raggedy Ann also had a secret, heartfelt wish. Raggedy Ann wished she could be a real girl. She hated never going anywhere but the toy box, Andy's room, and the garden. Raggedy Ann wanted to be real so she could explore. She wanted to see the world.

Sometimes Andy read her favorite stories to Raggedy Ann. One day she read from a book called *The Secret Garden*. In that book, the heroine finds an entrance to a secret garden and meets a magical boy who becomes her very special friend.

"Oh, if only I could find a secret garden," Andy yearned. "If only I could have a special friend."

And Raggedy Ann thought, "If I had a friend, maybe she would help me escape from here — if I were a real girl, that is."

That night Andy prayed, "Please send me a friend, please send me a friend."

And Raggedy Ann prayed, "Please make me a real girl. Please, please, please."

While she slept, that night in her dreams, Andy heard beautiful music and saw bright jewels made of many colors of sparkling light. Then, she saw a being of light who turned into a very kind-faced man.

"Are you an angel?" she asked.

"You may call me an angel, you may call me a guide, you may call me a teacher, or whatever you like — God has heard your prayers," said the man, "and because He loves you, He has sent me to you to give you the gift of friendship for which you have prayed."

"How?" asked Andy.

"I will make your doll, Raggedy Ann, a real girl," said the man. "If you can win her love before the week is gone, she will stay a real girl and she will always be your friend."

Meanwhile, the same beautiful, jeweled light and kind–faced man appeared to Raggedy Ann in her dreams. "Who are you?" she also asked.

"You may call me whatever you like," answered the kind–faced man, "God has sent me to grant you your wish. I will make you a real girl. If you can win the love of Andy before the week is gone, you may stay a real girl."

Saying this, the kind–faced man took a pure gold safety pin and pinned a red cloth heart to Raggedy Ann's chest. "When you have a heart, it means that you have the ability to choose. Make your choices well and you will stay real."

In Andy's dream, the kind–faced man said to her, "When you have a friend, you sometimes have to give up the things you want for the sake of your friendship.

Make your words and actions deserving of friendship and your friend will want to stay with you."

The next morning was Saturday. When Andy woke up, she ran to the toy box. There was Raggedy Ann, alive, pushing up the lid of the box and climbing out.

"My dream has come true. I can hardly believe it. It's so wonderful!" said Andy.

Raggedy Ann was thinking, "I can't believe it! I'm real! Now I can get away from that toy box and explore!"

Andy was thinking, "I'm so excited. I can't believe this is really happening. My doll is a real girl and now I'll have a friend."

"Hi!" said Raggedy Ann, "I'm hungry."

"So am I," said Andy. "Let's go downstairs and get some toast and milk." They both went down to the kitchen and Andy fixed some buttered toast and poured out two glasses of milk. They ate in silence, glancing from time to time out of the corners of their eyes at each other.

After breakfast, Andy said, "Raggedy Ann, I'm so glad you're alive! I've wanted a friend for so long. Let's play ping–pong."

"What?" said Raggedy Ann disdainfully, "Play ping–pong? How boring. Let's go downtown and see what's happening. I've always wanted to see something besides the toy box and the garden, and I think downtown would be a great place to start. You've never taken me anywhere and I can't wait to make up for lost time. Let's go!"

"Downtown?" exclaimed Andy. "That's miles and miles. And I don't know the way. But look, if you don't want to play ping–pong, let's do something else. Let's have a tea party."

"Tea party!" shrieked Raggedy Ann, "I'm sick of tea parties! I want adventure. I'm not just a doll any more and I don't have to do what you want. I can make my own choices now and I choose adventure!"

"But I don't like anything too scary," said Andy. "We might get hurt or get into trouble if we go too far by ourselves. I'll tell you what. Let's read *The Secret Garden* together and then ask Mrs. Brill for some juice and cookies."

"Garden, schmarden," yelled Raggedy Ann. "Don't you care what I want at all? Can't we at least go to the mall?"

By this time, Andy's face was bright red. "You're supposed to be my friend," she screamed. "And so you should do what I want. But you don't care what I want one bit, so you aren't a friend — you're just a darn old doll! And you're my doll! And I say we're going to play in the garden and that's that!" And Andy grabbed Raggedy Ann by the arm and dragged her towards the door.

Raggedy Ann jerked her arm out of Andy's grip. "I'm supposed to have my freedom," she screamed. "I wasn't made real so I could still be your doll and do whatever you say — I was made real so I could do what I want to do. And I'm not going to let you stop me!" Saying which she stepped out of the bedroom window, climbed down the trellis and walked rapidly down the driveway and away up the street.

Andy was in shock. She told Mrs. Brill she didn't feel well and went back to bed. She was worried something bad might happen to Raggedy Ann, but she was also angry about not getting her own way. "She always did exactly what I wanted when she was a doll," Andy thought. "I don't know what's gotten into her now that she's real."

Meanwhile Raggedy Ann was having a wonderful time. She hitched a ride to the biggest mall and there she went into all the shops, snuck into the movies, and rode up and down in the glass–walled elevator. At first, the other people at the mall thought she looked a bit odd, but then they figured she was wearing a costume and the red heart pinned to her chest was a club badge or something.

After a while, Raggedy Ann got thirsty. She saw a drinking fountain and drank to her heart's content. When she got hungry, she ate some chips and candy from free sample containers. At night, she hid inside the department store and slept in their furniture display bed.

Andy, however, felt lonelier than ever. And not

only lonely, but also angry. "That kind–faced man tricked me," she thought. "He was supposed to give me a friend — some friend. She didn't understand me or care about what I wanted at all."

And so the time went by.

One day, after reading *The Secret Garden* for a while, Andy thought, "I wonder if maybe it was really my fault? Was I acting like a spoiled brat? Was I selfish and bossy? Did I ever think about what Raggedy Ann felt like, just becoming real after a whole life of being someone's possession locked up in a box? Did I ever think even once of what she might want? The kind–faced man said having a friend meant sometimes not getting what I want, so I could give happiness to the person who was my friend. Did I ever think of that? No. I can see that being a friend is much harder than being a doll–owner, but oh, how I wish I could try again."

And Raggedy Ann also was thinking. By now, the streets and shops and movies were starting to seem really boring. And the chips and candy were making her feel sick to her stomach. She didn't want to go on living off free samples forever. And, she had to admit it, she felt lonely. "Is this what freedom is for?" she asked herself.

That night she watched a rerun of *E.T.* on the television set in the department store entertainment display. She saw how *E.T.* was different from the children and how he longed to be free and go home, but how he couldn't help being loving. "He always gave of himself to heal the children and make them happy," Raggedy Ann thought, "but I've used my freedom only to gain what I wanted for myself. The kind-faced man said I would have to make choices and whether I chose the right thing or the wrong thing would be up to me. Have I chosen the right things? Uh-oh, I don't think I have. I never thought about what Andy wanted at all. I never thought about making her happy, only about making myself happy. Why, she might be worried about me. And I'm lonely. I miss her. I want to go home."

The next morning as the sun was coming up, Andy heard a scratching sound at the window. She ran over to it. It was Raggedy Ann. Andy opened the window and Raggedy Ann climbed in. Andy hugged her.

"I've been so selfish," they both said at once. "No, really..." they both started again. Then they laughed and Andy spoke.

"Raggedy Ann, I'm so sorry. I never thought about you, only about me. We can go places. I'm sure my parents would adopt you and then we could go to summer camp together and take vacations in exciting places — Mrs. Brill could go with us. She's not very outgoing, but we'd have each other. Hey! I have an aunt in Chicago — we could go there for a weekend.

We can have such fun!"

"Wait, wait, wait," said Raggedy Ann. "I was wrong too. I was selfish. You know what I'd really like to do? I'd like to have a tea party in the garden. How about it?"

At that, Andy's face lit up with joy and the joy seemed to leap from her eyes to Raggedy Ann's heart. Then, Raggedy Ann understood what the kind–faced man had meant about choices.

"When I only wanted to satisfy my own desires," thought Raggedy Ann, "I never felt this happy. I thought freedom was for getting what I wanted, but now I know I was wrong. Now I know I can only be really happy if I use my freedom to give happiness to someone else as well as myself. I'm sure that choosing to make someone else happy is the right choice," she thought.

"Well," said Andy, "I'd love to have a tea party in the garden, if you want to, Raggedy Ann, but tonight maybe Mrs. Brill can take us to the mall for garden burgers and maybe we can see a movie at the Cinema or go bowling."

Then, smiling, they ran over and hugged each other tightly. Whereupon, they heard a jolly, laughing sound and looked around to see the kind–faced man smiling at them. "Why you're the man I saw in my dreams," Raggedy Ann and Andy both said at once.

"The week is gone," the kind–faced man said.

"And you both came through with flying colors. I was worried about you for awhile, but I counted on you to finally understand and you did. You understood that loving each other meant making some adjustments to each other's wishes and that freedom only means happiness when you use it for caring about others as well as yourself."

"So, one last thing, just to make it official," said the kind–faced man. "Do you, Andy, love Raggedy Ann?" he asked.

"Yes, I do," said Andy. "I love her more than my own selfishness."

"Then Raggedy Ann, you are a real girl forever. And Andy, you have become a friend so you will always have a friend."

Then the kind–faced man took the red cloth heart and golden safety pin from Raggedy Ann's chest and turned it into two golden heart–shaped lockets hanging from red velvet cords. He gave one to each of them saying, "Keep love in your hearts and you will always have a friend, and always be free."

The Snow Maiden

nce there was a girl who lived in a land where it was always winter. She was made of snow as were her seven brothers and sisters and, in fact, all of the people and animals who lived in Winterlong, for so the country was named. The maiden's name was Grayse. Her parents had named her after the winter sky which was always gray.

Once, Grayse asked her parents if there were countries in the world where there were other seasons besides winter.

"Yes," her mother said. "There are many."

"Yes," her father said. "In some it is almost always warm, and in some it is almost always rainy, but in all of them there are more seasons than one. Only here in Winterlong is it always winter."

"Has it always been this way?" asked Grayse.

Her mother and father looked at each other.

"You're too young, Grayse," said her mother.

"We'll talk about it when you're sixteen," said her father.

And no matter how carefully Grayse asked them or how often, that is all they would say.

Every day was just like the day before in Winterlong. Cold. Windy. Snowy. Icy. Since everything was always frozen, there were never any flowers. The trees were always bare. Of course, there was still beauty — the branches of the bare trees formed delicate patterns of lace against the gray sky. But it was a cold, hard beauty. Instead of green meadows, there were gray shadows cast by fields of drifting snow.

And it was so terribly cold. The ponds and rivers were always frozen. Sometimes where the largest river's rapids became a waterfall, the ice would thaw a little before refreezing. It was there that Grayse would go to sit and think, where the rippled patterns of dark water and snow-covered, frozen slush looked different from the endless snow and ice everywhere else.

She always sat so quietly that sometimes a pair of white Rock Doves would come and sit beside her. Their snowy, white plumage barely showed against the gray and white drifts around them. Only their black eyes and beaks stood out. They always seemed friendly as they sat there and watched the frozen patterns with her.

Sometimes Grayse would turn to them and ask, "Do you know a way to end this endless winter?" Although their dark eyes seemed to share her sadness, they never spoke. Grayse tried and tried, but she could never find anything written in any book or spoken by any teacher that gave her answers that really made sense to her.

Grayse always brought pieces of stale bread in her pocket for the doves. She thought they seemed to smile a little as she gave them the crumbs. She smiled too, to see them happy.

Then, one day, Grayse realized that seven years had passed since she'd spoken to her parents about the endless winter. The next day she would be sixteen. That evening she went to her parents.

"Mom, Dad," she said, "You promised you would tell me about the winter when I turned sixteen."

"Sit down, Grayse," said her dad.

"This is the story," said her mom. "All parents in Winterlong tell this story to their children on their sixteenth birthdays. We know that our children must be told the truth and we hope, perhaps, some day..." her voice trailed off sadly.

Grayse's dad took her mom's hand and continued, "We hope that some day a child will be born who will hear the truth, understand it, and find a way to set us free."

"Long, long ago," her dad continued, "so long that nobody can now say exactly how long, our country was just like all others in that it had more seasons than winter. We had a spring, summer and autumn also. Our people were not made of snow then but were just like all other people."

"Maybe not just like all others," said Grayse's mom. "Our people were perhaps a bit different because we knew so exactly what we wanted. We, or our ancestors actually, wanted wealth. And our ancestors were ready to do anything to get it."

"They worked hard," said Grayse's father. But they also schemed. They lied and cheated. They did not care who they hurt or what they did as long as they could make a profit. And they never tried to help anyone but themselves with their wealth."

"They took all the wealth they got and used it to build rich houses with rich furniture and beautiful carriages waiting outside in the carriage-ways," said Grayse's mom.

"Even when they had more than any sensible person could ever have wanted," said Grayse's dad, "they went on getting more and more and more. Their extra wealth was locked up in brass storerooms with big brass locks and guards on duty around the clock."

"Winterlong was the richest country on the earth at that time," said Mom, "but also the saddest. There were people living and dying on the streets. Some poor people didn't even have enough money to buy food or medicine. None of the wealthy people felt any obligation to help the people less fortunate than they. It wasn't wrong to work hard for things, but it was wrong to never, ever use any of the money they had to help people who were in desperate need. The misery of the poor was as hopeless as the pomp of the powerful was overdone."

"Then one day," said Dad, "on what would have been the first day of spring, the sun turned into pure gold, the moon into pure silver and the grass into emeralds. The sky turned into aquamarine, the rivers into hard crystal, and the lakes into diamond. The leaves turned into paper money and blew away as a fierce and icy wind started blowing. That wind froze all of the people of Winterlong into snowmen and snow-women."

"When the people tried to flee the icy wind and frozen wasteland," continued Mom, "they discovered that if they crossed the country's boundaries, they melted and were gone. Thus it was that nobody could leave. It was then the country was named Winterlong, and it has been endless winter ever since."

"Still, every time a child is born, we know hope," said her dad.

"We hope that the child will grow up to be wiser than we were or are," said Grayse's mother, looking very sad.

Grayse hugged them both, kissed them good night and went to her bed. Before she went to sleep she thought and thought. "Each time a child is born, there is hope," she thought. "What is it that gives us the ability to hope?"

The next morning, as Grayse wakened to the day of her sixteenth birthday, all of a sudden she thought "love." She laughed out loud and ran to the window and looked out. Was there a glimmer, for a moment, of a blue sparkle in the gray sky?

"It is love," she thought. "When a child is born, all people feel love. It's love that gives us hope, and hope that gives us more love. When people tell their children about Winterlong, they are telling them because they hope their children will have better lives than they have and that also is love. It was greed and lack of love that drove the other seasons away. Maybe giving and love can bring them back."

Grayse dressed quickly and ran to her favorite spot by the frozen river's rapids where the waterfall's waves lay chained by the ice and snow.

The Rock Doves greeted her and she smiled at them as she gave them the bread chunks and crumbs she kept for them in her pocket.

"I think there is a power behind the snow and the wind and the sky," she said to the two birds, who looked up at the sound of her voice. "I think some creative force made us all and everything else as well and keeps it all going, so the earth doesn't burn in the light of the sun or the sky dissolve into the stars."

Grayse looked out at the frozen water and barren, bleak fields of snow and felt hope warming her heart. "When we turned to greed," she said to the doves, "we fell out of harmony, and brought this endless winter upon ourselves. But I think whoever created us all has kept love alive in our hearts, waiting for us to turn away from greed and selfishness. I think if I ask for help with faith in love I will be heard."

"So I will," Grayse whispered to herself, "I ask you — whoever you may be — in the name of love — to help us learn to live in harmony again."

There was a booming sound like thunder as the waterfall started to break free from the ice that bound it. "Does anyone hear me?" Grayse whispered even more softly.

"Yes, Grayse," said a sweet voice. And Grayse looked up to see a being who looked like an angel in front of her. The angel was surrounded with light, and her eyes looked like stars. White wings with feathers that glittered and sparkled lay folded neatly just showing from behind her shoulders and head.

"Who are you?" asked Grayse.

"I am sent from that Power which created all that is — from our Creator," the angel said in a voice like a joyful song. "I am the spirit of love, joy, friendship, peace, kindness, helping, sharing, caring and goodness for all the earth and all the creation upon it. I am the spirit of love for all and all for love. You called for help and our Creator sent me."

"Can you help us?" asked Grayse.

"Yes," sang the angel with eyes full of warmth,

smiling. "I will tell spring, summer and fall to visit your land again but you must tell your parents and your brothers and sisters, and all the folk of your land to honor love for all in their thoughts, words and deeds, and you must do so as well.

"Those who are willing to start learning to live with love will see the spring unfolding and feel the warmth of peace and joy in their hearts. But listen well — if there are those who will not learn, they will still only see and feel winter."

"That sounds beautiful," said Grayse. "But a lot of people have lived the opposite way all their lives. What can I say that will show us what honoring love in our thoughts, words and deeds means — how to actually do it?"

"Tell everyone to think of themselves as trading places with every other person or creature they see," the angel said. "If you try to imagine yourself in another person's situation, it will be easier to understand what you can say or do that will be kind and helping. If something would make you feel better or happier in that person's place, then do it! If something would make you feel worse or sadder, then don't do it. It's really that simple," she said, vibrations of happiness spreading out around her as her wings unfolded for a moment looking like white velvet, covered with rainbow-hued sequins.

"Do you mean like when I saw the doves by the

waterfall and they looked cold and sad and hungry so I brought them crumbs because I thought it might make them happier?" asked Grayse.

"YES! That's exactly what I mean," cried the angel actually lifting with joy into the air. "How did you know they would like the crumbs?" she asked, settling lightly down again.

"I just thought they might. I thought I would if all my food was covered up with snow and hard to get. And when I put the crumbs on the ground, they sort of perked up and they pecked it all up so quickly. Then they cleaned their feathers and sat there looking relaxed and really happy."

"How did it make you feel when you saw them looking happier?" the angel asked, her wings fluttering just a little, sending rainbow light reflections dancing on the snow where she stood.

"It made me feel wonderful!" answered Grayse. "That's why I do it every day now even when we don't have a lot of bread ourselves."

"So you do understand," said the angel looking as if heaven had just that moment come to earth.

"But what if the other person's situation is too hard to fix?" asked Grayse. "What if I see something I should do but fail at doing it? If we fail, will we still be frozen?"

"Our Creator knows our hearts," the angel said. "Nobody can be perfect except the Creator. But if you sincerely wish to help rather than hurt, that intention will guide you. Once you start thinking of how to make others happy and what would be helping and caring, it will be easier to see and easier to do. The important thing is to really want to change and really try to do it. If you do that, little by little you *will* change, and it will happen naturally and

gradually. Soon you will be happy and you will make the people around you happy too."

"Thank you!" Grayse said. And, as she said 'thank you,' the snow she was formed of began to melt and her heart to lift and her eyes to sparkle. Soon she was completely unfrozen. She ran to the angel and hugged her tightly.

Then the angel spoke, and her words were like a song of tinkling bells. "Your name was Grayse because the sky was gray, but now the sky is blue again and white clouds sail there and rainbows signal the glory of our Creator's love for all that lives on earth. As you have changed from ice and snow, your name also will change and from now onwards will be Grace."

And hand in hand, joyous and laughing, Grace and the rainbow-velvet-winged angel walked through the wakening, blossoming fields to tell Winterlong that spring had come.

The Wizard and the Wicked Witch

nce there was a wonderful wizard who lived in the village of West Wood. He was an old, old man who had meditated so long that he had become one with God and nature. But if you met him, you might not see his oneness, you might see only his kindness and his wisdom.

In fact, it was his wisdom that made the local villagers decide to call him wizard. "What should we call you?" they asked him.

"Call me brother, father, uncle, teacher, call me anything," the wizard said "for no matter what you call me, I will be what I am." But the villagers, who loved him for his kindness and respected him for his wisdom, always called him wizard.

He lived alone in a small cottage on the edge of the forest. He built the cottage himself of strong oak with a fieldstone hearth and foundation. His windows were of the green-tinted glass produced in the village of East Wood and the roof was finished with cedar. Flowering vines grew all over the cottage — rose vines on the south and west walls, trumpet vines on the east wall and clematis on the north. Birds of all sorts nested in the eaves, and squirrels and chipmunks carried fallen walnuts and hazelnuts from his trees to bury in the flower beds next to his front door. All the wild creatures sensed his kindness and purity and seemed to take comfort in being close to where he lived.

Every day he prayed and meditated, tended his herb, vegetable and flower gardens, and helped whatever person, plant or animal needed him most. Sometimes it was a tree hit by blight. Sometimes it was a sick deer or dog, a wounded bird, or a needy person.

He wanted to use his wisdom for helping people rather than for fame or fortune, so he invited the villagers to call on him freely if they needed him. He never took money for himself in exchange for his help. He lived on what he grew in his garden. But sometimes the villagers gave him money to help those in need — widows, orphans, or sick people living all alone — because the villagers knew he would use the money wisely.

In addition to helping others any way he could, the wizard taught anyone who asked how to meditate on the inner Light. "Inner Light is a gift of God like sunshine, air and water," he often said. "It is the birthright God has given freely to everyone, so all can have the peace and joy it gives."

After school the village children usually went to his forest home and helped him with his garden or his chores. Afterwards, they would practice meditation, and then the wizard would tell them wonderful stories and give them sweet tea and cookies. They would sit together in the flower garden in the spring and summer, on the back porch in the fall, and around the cozy hearth with a warm fire crackling in the winter.

The children loved his stories. The wizard was delightful and spoke with a twinkling, joyful humor as well as wisdom. Sometimes his stories were funny, sometimes they were sad, but they always gently taught the virtues of kindness, of sharing with others and caring for others, of being honest and being good.

One day, Maya the Merciless, a very wicked witch was roaming around looking for trouble. She saw the village of West Wood. She saw that people there lived simple, contented lives and this bothered her. It worked but it wasn't orderly. She liked to take charge of things and make them run properly. When she was in control, things were done right, she felt. She hung around for several days trying to find some way to move in and take over.

One day she was sneaking around next to the wizard's cottage, when she smelled the delicious fragrance coming from the sweet tea and cookies. She snuck up close to see what was going on.

She heard the children laughing with delight and saw them smiling with joy. When she saw them hugging the wizard as they said good-bye, she felt a terrible pain overtake her. Normally the witch was so busy thinking nasty thoughts and doing mean things that she didn't notice anything else. But now, somehow, she felt the pain of overpowering loneliness. It was her soul wishing that she, too, could love and be loved, but she had no idea how to be loving or, in fact, that she even had a soul.

"That wizard feeds them tea and cookies," she thought. "Well, I'll feed them ice cream and cake and then they'll hug and kiss me."

So she swooped down on the children, cast a spell upon them, and carried them off to her castle. There she bid them sit on the stony, hard ground and fed them ice cream and little frosted cakes.

But the children were frightened of her. She smelled terrible and a black fog created by all her negative thoughts hung around her. The cakes and ice cream looked good, but the witch didn't smile when she handed them out. "Eat your ice cream!" she commanded them. Of course, since she was commanding them to do something, the children didn't want to do it, so they didn't.

"I'm in charge here!" the witch said in a stern voice. "Now eat your ice cream and then give me a hug." At this, the children started crying. The witch was furious. "What does that wizard have that I don't?" she wondered.

When the children wouldn't touch the ice cream

and just kept on crying, the witch told them she'd give them a few days to come to their senses, but if they didn't eat by the end of the week she'd make them sorry. Then, muttering under her breath grumpily, she sent them all to locked rooms in the castle.

Meanwhile, the children didn't come to visit the wizard as they usually did. The wizard missed them but went on with his chores. When they didn't come the day after, or the day after that, the wizard was worried. He closed up his cottage and walked to the village to find out if they were all right.

As he walked through the village, the wizard saw that all the houses, fields and shops were empty. "Where is everyone?" he wondered. Then, he saw Spot, a black and white puppy whose broken leg the wizard had set and healed. Spot barked and barked.

"Hey, Spot," said the wizard, "where is everybody?"

Spot barked again and pointed with his nose to the center of town.

"Okay, boy," said the wizard and followed Spot to the Town Hall. He asked Spot to wait outside, opened the door and walked in. As soon as the door closed behind him, people ran up, all of them shouting all at once.

"Wait, wait," he said. "One at a time so I can hear you. Muriel, why don't you tell me what's wrong?"

"Three days ago, in the morning when we woke up, we noticed a thin black fog," said Muriel. "The next day the fog was thicker, darker and smelled like spoiled garbage. We were all afraid.

"This morning," she continued, "the fog was gone but so were the children. Every single person under eighteen-years old was gone. Disappeared. All that was left was a bad smell."

"This sounds serious," said the wizard.

"What do you think it is?" asked Jenny.

"I think it's the wicked witch," said the wizard. "Long ago, when the world was young, a wicked witch wanted to gain control of all creation. She wanted power more than anything else! She learned magic so she could bend everyone and everything to her will. She rampaged over all the earth conquering and controlling. All the people of the earth prayed to God for help against her evil. He heard their prayers and banished the witch to the other side of the world. But God knew that even someone as evil as the witch had a soul and therefore one spark of goodness. Because of this, He did not destroy her. He hoped that one day she would learn how to love and leave her evil ways. I'm afraid she's left her banishment and stolen your children."

"Can anyone find her?" asked Muriel.

"And can anyone save the children?" asked Billy.

"I will go," said the wizard. "And if it's God's will, the children and I will return."

"Bless you wizard," they all cried out. "Our hearts

and our prayers will be with you."

So the wizard started off.

"But it's night," said Muriel. "Can't you wait till morning?"

"There is no night where there is Light," said the wizard and, waving to them all, started off to the other side of the world.

He hadn't gone thirty feet before he heard something crashing behind him. It was Spot kicking up leaves with his paws, and barking with a hopeful look.

"Okay, Spot," said the wizard. "You can come, too."

Spot barked happily and they started off together walking mile after mile, till night turned into day and day into night and then into day again. By this time Spot was so tired the wizard had to carry him. But he wasn't very heavy and he made happy, little snorting puppy sounds snuggled softly in the wizard's arms.

On the fourth day of travel, Spot wrinkled up his nose and yipped in disgust. "Yes, Spot," said the wizard. "I think we're getting close to her."

On the fifth day the smell was almost unbearable and that afternoon a black fog started to obscure the sun. As the fog got thicker and thicker, the wizard stopped.

"Okay Spot," he said, "The love of God is the strongest force in the whole universe. And the next strongest force is the love we have for each other. We are seeing the darkness created by hatred, greed and anger — if we hate back it will only strengthen the darkness."

Spot gave a short, approving bark.

"We can fight the darkness of the witch's deeds, but we must pity the witch herself," the wizard said. She is filled with the misery that hatred brings. Our only hope lies in sticking to love. If we do that — some day — she'll get just one bit of its sweetness and the darkness in her heart will start to lessen."

As he spoke, light glowed softly all around him. "There is no night where there is Light," he said.

Spot barked softly.

Then, seeing their path by the Light surrounding the wizard, they walked up to the castle of the wicked witch.

"Who goes there?" a high and crackling voice called out.

"It is I, the Wizard of West Wood," said the wizard.

"Woof," said Spot.

"This is the castle of Maya the Merciless," said the witch, "Be gone!"

"But we have come for the children of West Wood," said the wizard.

"Be gone before I burn you into soot and cinders," said the witch.

"Light also burns," said the wizard. "The candle

flame burns the wick. The cooking fire burns the fuel and the sun burns so that we can have warmth and daylight. As there is warmth in fire, there is also light. By Light I beseech you, let us see the children."

"I am Maya the Merciless, but I am also Maya the Mighty. See them you may and then — be gone or beware."

Whereupon the wizard and Spot found themselves inside the castle walls. They were in a large yard and all the children were there sitting on the cold, hard ground with plates of ice cream and frosted cakes in front of them. They looked terribly unhappy and some of the younger ones were crying.

"It's okay, children," he called to them, "don't despair. Find the Light within you. You know how."

"That's enough," screamed the witch and blasted the children with fog. But, to her horror, the dark fog stopped short of Spot, the wizard, and the children. Each of them was surrounded by a Light the darkness could not touch.

"Please, dear Maya," said the wizard, "set them free."

"I won't let them go until they love me!" screamed the witch and hurled fire and brimstone at them. But the Light held and none of the children or Spot or the wizard were harmed.

"Maya," said the wizard, "these children will never belong to you. You can shout at them all you want but your anger will never get you what you really wish for. Until you yourself are loving, nobody will love you. And no matter how much you try to control them, they won't do what you want without love. Admit it. They belong to the Light. What good can they do you?"

"Love-shove. Who cares about love? Not me!" the witch screeched. "But it's true — they're filled with that cursed Light. I thought maybe they'd forget, but then you came along. You're right. They're no good to me at all. Make me an offer. If the price is right, maybe..."

"But I own nothing, Maya," said the wizard. "I can't pay you anything."

"Then give me the dog," screamed the witch. "A tasty puppy will be a super supper treat."

Spot put his paws over his eyes and howled in fear.

"Don't worry, Spot," said the wizard, "the Light is around you too. She can't touch you."

"Well," said the witch, "if you have nothing to bargain with, then get out! I can't touch the children, but I can certainly make them miserable." And her evil, cackling laugh filled the air, as black flakes of soot rained down on them, each flake spreading a rank, polluted odor.

"Maya," said the wizard. "Have you forgotten that some day you will die?"

"Are you threatening me?" screamed the witch.

"No," said the wizard. "It's a fact. Everything that lives will some day die. Since you are alive, that includes you. And then you will go to God and you will see all your good deeds and all your bad deeds brought before you. You know this is true."

"So?" squinted the witch.

"When you face God, do you hope for justice or for mercy, forgiveness and love?" asked the wizard.

"I am Maya the Merciless. How can I hope for mercy, forgiveness and love?" sighed the witch.

"Justice will give you the amount of suffering you have caused to others," said the wizard. "Only forgiveness and love will give you peace."

"But I have been so very wicked. I could never deserve forgiveness and love," said the witch.

"Nobody deserves forgiveness and love," said the wizard. "It is always a gift. Because God is our Father and loves us."

"I could never get that gift," said the witch, scowling. But then, looking up almost hopefully, she whispered, "Could I?"

"God's forgiveness is for everyone. He is a loving Father. But if you want to experience the warmth of His forgiveness and love, you must try sincerely to give the same love you want to all His children whenever and however you can."

"So I guess you're saying I'd have to let the children go?" asked the witch.

"That's right," said the wizard, nodding his head.

"And I would have to let that delicious–looking little puppy walk away uncooked?" whined the witch.

"Yes," said the wizard.

"Oh, all right!" the witch growled. She kicked the ground till it burst into smoky flames and she waved her arms till sparks flew. Then she calmed down and said, "I can barely believe it, but I have to agree. You win. Get those wretched brats and that flea–bitten dog out of my sight. Those rotten children were nothing but trouble anyway. Take them and get out!" And she flew off in a shower of sooty sparks and the children were free.

And so the wizard won not only the freedom of the children of West Wood, but also the salvation of the wicked witch. For, little by little, Maya found that kindness brought her more happiness than wickedness, and she became more and more kindly and merciful as the years went by. Finally, towards the end of her life, she turned half her castle into low-cost apartments for poor people and one-fourth into an orphanage and the other one-fourth into an up-to-date dispensary for people who couldn't afford medical care. She spent all her spare time helping the sick, the orphans or anyone else who needed her. She even finally learned to meditate from the wizard himself, and spent several hours each day in meditation on the inner Light. Ultimately she became known as Mother Maya and was surrounded by a community of people she had helped, all of whom loved her very much.

As for the wizard, he gathered the children around him, the older ones carrying the younger ones and he carrying Spot, and they turned their steps towards the other side of the world and marched home, singing:

> *You can't go wrong*
> *when you go right.*
> *There is no dark*
> *where there is Light.*

> *Find your heart,*
> *make each a friend.*
> *Follow the Light,*
> *all wrong will mend.*

> *You can't go wrong*
> *when you go right.*
> *There is no dark*
> *where there is Light.*

A Rainbow Needs All Its Colors

Some time after God first created rainbows, they got tired of appearing on earth and then disappearing into the ether. They asked God if they could have a city just for themselves in heaven, so they wouldn't have to disappear after returning from earth and God agreed. Soon all the rainbows moved to their very own city and established households there.

The city became a lovely place. We on earth see just a few colors when we see a rainbow. Actually every hue, shade and tint in infinity exists within the rainbow's glorious possibilities. Soon all of those bright and beautiful colors came to live in Rainbow City. The colors married each other, had children, built and decorated homes, and spent their off-work hours creating paintings, ballets, symphonies and poems of color. It was quite a lovely life for everyone concerned.

A few thousand years passed by. Many colors had been on earth delighting humanity as rainbows in the sky. Unfortunately, quite a few of those colors started picking up some of the lower habits they saw on earth.

One day Purple called a meeting. Many colors

attended. They thought Purple would have a new poem or painting. But instead Purple said "I am the best color. My ancestors created the royal purple of Roman togas. I demand to be recognized as your empress or I will remove the color purple from any rainbow that appears on earth."

Of course, the rest of the colors were terribly upset, but declaring one color as empress seemed rather silly when all had been created equal and given equal love by God. So they refused. From that time on, purple was no longer seen in the rainbows appearing in the skies of earth.

Next, Yellow-green called a meeting. "I am not popular on earth," she said. "I feel unappreciated and unloved, so I've decided to quit." And from that time yellow-green was not seen in the rainbows that graced earth skies.

Then it was Orange. "I'm the best of all of you," he said. "I'm the hottest thing around. I pep everything up! None of you admits how much more important my color is in the rainbow display. I'm the most important color in the sunset also. Either you treat me like I'm the best color around, or I'm quitting too."

Most of the other colors didn't know how to treat anybody differently. God had told them at the very beginning to treat each other with love and that is what they had been doing. They couldn't imagine how to treat one color with more love because that would mean they would have to treat the others with less. So Orange quit and was no more seen in the skies of earth.

One horrible day, Magenta threw a fit. "You're all talking about me. I know you are. You're talking about me behind my back. You're saying I'm ugly and deformed and out of style. You're saying my color is the color of scars and bruises. I can't take it any more!" She ran away and took her part of the rainbow with her.

Yellow was next. "I don't get enough praise. You're always arguing with me. Don't you realize I'm more intelligent than any of you? I understand things better. My education and intelligence make my ideas totally superior! Why don't you treat me properly? People should listen to everything I say with appreciation for my superior intelligence, wit and excellence. Well, until I get the respect I deserve I won't make any further appearances." So yellow was gone from the rainbows appearing in earth skies.

Now only Blue, Green and Red were left.

One terrible day, Green and Red stood hand in hand while Green gave a statement the two of them had prepared. "Red and green have never been really popular," Green said. "The only time people bring us out is at Christmas time and then we're used in such boring, corny ways. We must not have any real value or people would care about us all the time. We're very depressed. People don't like us and we're going away where we won't have to see anybody. We feel bad every time we see how well other colors are treated, and how we're always left out. Good-bye." And, weeping, Red and Green left. Now their colors were gone from the rainbows of earth as well.

Finally only Blue was left. Blue had always been a steadfast color. His nickname, after all, was 'True Blue.' But even though Blue still appeared in the rainbows of earth, with Blue all by himself, it was hard to tell him from the sky.

The people of earth started to notice that there were no more rainbows. Children looked at pictures of rainbows in stories and wondered what they were. Parents remembered the rainbows they used to see and tried to tell their children what they had been like. Secretly, they worried that rainbows were gone forever. Scientists said the disappearance of rainbows was due to global warming and the hole in the ozone layer. Those people who had the most faith prayed to God.

One day in Rainbow City, God went to Blue. "I've been receiving so many letters, phone calls and prayers about missing rainbows," said God. "Can you tell me what happened?" (Of course, God always knows everything but, being the most loving and humble of all, He often acts as if He doesn't.)

Blue told God all that had happened. God was

very upset. "I created rainbows as a sign of my love for all," He said. "I created all colors equal and gave all of you everything. All I wanted was for you to love each other." Then God called all the colors together. Everybody was there, even those colors that had quit playing their parts in the rainbows.

"Some of you think you're more special. Some of you think you're less special," God said. "The truth is that all of us are equal! It is God's Light inside each of us that makes us all equal. Every single color has something of value to give to my creation.

"When you learn to give the most importance to God's Light, you'll see it within yourself as well as in others. If you practice looking for it you'll see it sooner. When you learn to treat everyone as equally special, you'll be happy and you'll make others happy, too."

Then God looked at all the colors of the rainbow as they stood in vast multitudes gathered before him and He smiled. He gazed at them and such divine love, bliss and joy came from His eyes that it filled their hearts. Soon, all of the colors started to smile. Then, they started hugging each other. They started dancing around and around. Soon the very air was dancing and the colors themselves were in ecstasy. They all felt only love and saw only beauty.

The people of earth looked up in wonder at the sky as it filled with sparkling, dazzling, radiant rainbows as far as eyes could see.

The rainbows, the sky, the heavens and the earth were singing, and time itself stood still. It was all rainbow-colored, shining, radiant light as all creation sang, "Let us all love each other and the cup of His Love go round and round and round forever!" 🖌

Little Lizard

On the edge of a great forest, there lived a little lizard. He was ugly and slow even for a lizard. He was not an appealing creature. He had no useful skills, nor was he especially virtuous. In fact, there was nothing special about him at all.

One day he heard a fast-flying hawk tell a falcon of a pond it had heard of in the middle of the forest which was owned by a great Lord renowned for his beauty and kindness.

"The pond is so clear," the hawk said, "that it reflects the sun by day and the moon by night. If you can find it and bathe in its waters, all the filth of the forest falls away and you are filled with an indescribable joy and peace in which you can stay forever."

"Really?" said the falcon. "Let's find it!" And they flew away.

"I would like to go there also," thought the lizard, "though it sounds like it would be hard work. It would take so long and probably be very difficult. Probably I wouldn't do very well, but, yes — I will go." And he started bravely off towards the middle of the forest.

He traveled and traveled and traveled, living on the food he could find on the way. The delicate pads of his tiny feet got sore walking and he always felt tired. He never seemed to make any progress towards getting anywhere and he often felt discouraged and sad.

Years went by. Sometimes companions joined him and for a while he felt less lonely, but they always left and then he was alone again, trudging on towards a destination he could barely remember.

After more years had passed, Little Lizard found he had almost lost hope. Still, he kept plodding and dragging on towards the pond he had heard of so long ago. Sometimes he almost forgot why he was walking, but then a shaft of sunlight would slant down through the leaves of the trees of the forest and he would remember what had inspired him to start upon this journey that was taking so much longer than he had ever dreamed it would.

One day, he looked at himself in a rain puddle and saw that his face had gotten old and full of wrinkles. His scales had become gray and many were missing. He looked blotched and patchy. "I'm old," he thought, and began to lose all hope.

That same day, as he was plodding and dragging — still forward — though full of grim sadness that felt like despair, he heard a voice. It came from a man with the kindest eyes he had ever seen. The man beckoned to him, so Little Lizard stopped and listened.

"Little Lizard, where are you going?" asked the man. Little Lizard was too tired to even wonder how the man could know his name. "I have heard," he answered wistfully, "that there is a pond in the middle of the forest which is so clear that it reflects the sun by day and the moon by night and that if you bathe in the waters of that pond, all the mud and filth of the forest fall away and you are filled with an indescribable joy and peace in which you can stay forever."

The man reached down and picked up Little Lizard. He paid no attention to the mud that covered him, but hugged him and petted him. Little Lizard closed his tired eyes and remembered how his mother had loved him in their nest so long ago. He nestled against the kind man's chest and felt a joy and peace he had never experienced before.

"Yes, I know of that pond," said the man. "In fact I am traveling there myself. At the rate at which you are going it will probably take you thousands of lifetimes to reach there. I can get there faster. Would you like to come with me?"

"Oh, yes," Little Lizard replied. And the man, full of gentle warmth, took the lizard into his own power, into his own love. And as he did, one sparkling tear of compassion fell from his eyes and splashed onto the

lizard's back. As it touched him, all the filth and mud fell away and Little Lizard was clean and dry and cozy.

"Little Lizard," said the man, "I am the Lord of the pond you seek; the pond is made from the tears I shed for all creatures great and small. Beautiful or ugly, good or bad, they are all mine and I love them. Some find me more quickly, some more slowly, but since you seek me now and have traveled so long, I have come to you."

And he hugged the little lizard tight within his arms, tucking him sweetly next to his heart, saying "Let us now go home."

Catkin

Once a proud and pretty cat lay on pillows, lay on blankets, lay on cushions, looked out windows, lapped up cream, and slept her days away.

Then the High King, Lord of Faery, took all the places she had lain on, hid all the spaces she had stayed in, and turned her life all upside down. Now she had no place to rest. Now she had to leave her homeland.

You see, he loved her very much, and he knew that if she simply went on sleeping she would never start her journey. But if she never started out, she would never ever find him, and he knew she loved him best, because she had seen him once, and any mortal — cat or queen — who saw but once the Faery King, could never, in their heart of hearts, truly love another.

And so the catkin, sore of heart, walked and walked through day and night, hill and vale, winter and summer, east and west and north and south.

And as the catkin went on walking,
to herself she started talking.
She missed her home so very badly;
she felt its loss so very sadly.

"How will I ever reach the King,
now that I've lost everything?"

Just then she saw his shining face —
the Faery King, off just a pace.
He knelt down and pulled her near.
"Little Catkin, little dear,
Listen now to what I say
and know I'll not be far away.
Every morning and at night,
close your eyes and see God's Light.
For this inner Light you see
will help you on your way to me.
And please remember most of all —
it's more important to be small
than it is to be too tall.
It's more important to be kind
than to have the smartest mind.
Think of everyone you see
as in a disguise that's hiding me.
I am there in each you meet —
so smile at everyone you greet.
When you're kind to all at last,
you will journey very fast."

When Catkin stopped to take her rest, she wept as she remembered her home, her blankets and her dinners of cream. Then she smiled to think of her recent visit from the Faery King but frowned as she thought about what he had said. What did he mean? What was she supposed to do? She was a show cat. Her ancestors for generations had been champions. She was better than others. How could she help it if it showed? How could she help it if her breeding, qualities and education placed her above so many? Was it her fault that she was different from the many ugly, common, boring and stupid creatures in the world?

Finally she slept. In the morning she groomed her paws and face and was horrified to find a sort of sticky dirt covering her fur that she couldn't seem to get off. Trying to clean her fur took so much time she decided not to close her eyes and look for the Light within. She was late. She had places to go. She would definitely do it tomorrow, she thought, and started off.

Just as she was prancing out,
a turtle came, a silly lout.

"I'm new in town," the turtle said.
"Well, that is really just too bad,"
Catkin rather meanly said. "It's sort of sad,
but there surely might be danger

in talking to a lonely stranger.
Even though the sun's out bright
and you look okay, you really might
be weird, or loud, or torrid,
or crazy, or somehow horrid.
If I tried to talk a bit
you might shout, or stutter or spit.
I can't talk to any peasant —
what if it turned out unpleasant?"

And so she turned her face away
and walked past him with naught to say.

That day she walked and walked but seemed to get nowhere. When she stopped at night to rest she found only a small bare patch of dirt upon which to lie. All the other ground for miles around was covered with briars and brambles. There was nothing to eat and, as she tried to sleep, she was bothered by a very unpleasant odor.

"Peiaoou!" she said the next morning when, to her horror, she found the smell came from the sticky coating of dirt all over her fur. She tried to lick and even bite the dirt away but no matter how hard she tried, it wouldn't come off.

"I think I'd better try to see that inner Light the Faery King told me about," she thought. She curled her tail neatly around, tucked her four paws beneath her and closed her eyes. Yes, there was a sort of dim glow before her inner eye. She tried to look at it, but it was so boring. Pretty soon she quit, stretched herself and started walking.

Two birds then came walking by.
"Catkin, have you seen the sky?"
"No," she said. "Not for a minute,
will I waste my time on a loon and linnet.
A crazy and a stupid bird —
a sillier thing I've never heard.
What could they say I need to know —
I can't be bothered — I have to go,
for one of breeding and high state
must guard her time — I can't be late."

That day Catkin walked and walked but again didn't seem to get anywhere. At night when she stopped to rest, the dirt on her fur was even stickier and smelled even worse. She licked and scrubbed and cleaned but it wouldn't budge.

"Oh how will I ever get clean?" she thought. "And how will I find the country of the Faery King and how will I ever cross the distance between us?"

The next morning she looked at the inner Light as the King had told her she should. Again it was dim and boring. She was about to give up in disgust when she thought, "After all, it was the Faery King himself who told me to do this. He said it would help me. There must be something to what he said — maybe if I tried harder to look more steadily and to keep my tail from thrashing around I would see more." She tried again and this time the Light did seem brighter and she felt a little peace within herself.

She ate some tender, new green grass for breakfast, drank some puddle water and started on her way.

A chubby badger, tiresome too,
said "Catkin, Catkin, is that you?"

"That fat, old badger has nothing to say,"
thought Catkin in her usual way.
"Not now. Tomorrow — no, next week,"
she said and tried to sneak
away. "Please," the badger said, so dreary.
"Can't you see I'm rather weary?"
said Catkin thinking "If I'm clever
I won't be talking to him ever."

That night her dirty fur seemed to smell quite terrible. "Could that smell really be coming from me?" she thought in horror but then decided, "No — absolutely not." As she went to sleep she had to admit that she hadn't covered any distance at all that day either.

The next morning, after trying to clean her fur and failing, she settled down with her tail curled around her for warmth. Was the Light even dimmer than before? "Am I doing something wrong?" she thought as she set out on her way.

As she was going along quite well,
she suddenly sniffed a repulsive smell.

"A stinky skunk!" she exclaimed.

III

A little skunk wept tears of shame.
"Won't anyone ever say my name
with love?" he cried. "I would,
if I could, always smell good.
I can't help that I smell bad.
Please understand it makes me sad.
Look at you — you're so grand,
won't you try to understand?
If, at least, you understood,
then maybe others also would."

"I really don't know why I should,"
Catkin said. "I've important stuff to do.
I can't be bothered with the likes of you."
She left the skunk in tears of pain.
"I haven't gone very far again,"
said Catkin as she closed her eyes.
In dream the Faery King, so wise,
said "You're the slowest cat I've ever seen.
You're not only proud, you're also mean.
At this rate you're so far behind,
you'll never make it in this lifetime.
 I've told you once, I've told you twice,
that you must learn to be really nice.
You cannot hope to stay the same
if you want to win this game.
All are special and all are dear —
you must attempt to see it clear.
If you hurt any, you hurt me.
If you're so smart, why can't you see?"

"This is the way I have to be.
I cannot change for this is me."

"No, my Catkin sweet and strong,
you think it's you but you are wrong.
You are just the same as me —
when you fully want to be."

"Please then, sir, so full of grace,
help me change my wicked ways."

"When you pray from your heart,
grace will come and change will start,"
said the King, bowing low.
"Goodbye for now. I must go."

That night Catkin found nothing to eat and only some water thick with mud from a smelly, rotting swamp to drink. She cried as she remembered her home and cried harder still when she thought of what the Faery King had said. "I've been full of pride and acted so mean. But even though I finally begin to see how bad I've been, will I be able to change now just because I want to? And will I ever be able to get my fur clean?"

The next morning the inner Light seemed brighter and easier to look at. When she cleaned her fur the dirt was less thick. For the first time since starting out on her journey she didn't feel heartbroken and homesick. She actually felt hopeful as she ate a bit of catnip she had stumbled upon and then started out.

Slowly she walked along and only
God Himself knew how lonely
she felt as she went on walking.

"I'm so lonely I'd even like talking
to that little skunk," she thought,
as, to her horror, she felt herself caught.

Catkin had stepped onto a hunter's forgotten trap.
The snare had looped around her leg and jerked her
up into the air. Helplessly, she hung by her left hind
paw, twisting slowly in the slight breeze that blew
through the leaves of the oak tree to which the upper
end of the hunter's snare was attached. From time to
time she tried desperately to raise herself up high
enough to chew through the rope which bound her,
but she couldn't do it no matter how hard she tried.
She was helpless and the weight of her body hanging
was starting to hurt very badly.

"How I wish someone would come to help me,"
she thought. "But who would? I long for help with all
my heart, but did I ever help anyone? No. Did I ever
do anything for anyone? No. So why would anyone
help me, even if they did come along?"

So from a hunter's forgotten snare,
she hung by the paw and cried, "I care
a lot now for the pain I gave,
because it's kindness I also crave.
I see that I was proud and mean.
If only truly I could have been
nicer then when the King told me how.

I beg God above for mercy now.
Forgive me all the pain I caused
and grant me kindness just because
You are all Love — You are all Light.
Please, by Your grace, make me all right."

Just then she caught a certain smell.
"Catkin, are you doing well?"
said the skunk, himself, no less.
"Oh Skunk, I ask the Lord to bless
your dear self for coming near —
could you help me down from here?"

He gnawed the rope with his teeth;
soon Catkin was free and, in relief,
said, "I insulted you before,
now I wish to even that score.
Is there something I can do
to ease the pain I gave to you?"

"Come with me please, Catkin, do.
For one day's journey be my friend."
They walked together and, at the end
of a long and very peaceful day,
Catkin saw a castle not far away.

"It is the castle of the Faery King,"
said Skunk. "I'm glad to bring

you here. This is the gift that I give free
to whoever has loved me unselfishly."

That night as Catkin cleaned her fur there was much less dirt and the smell was gone. She felt very much at peace and ate a bit of cheese Skunk had given her for supper quite happily. She stretched full out and, resting her paws over her eyes, fell into sleep wherein she dreamed of the Faery King standing near her. He was looking at her so lovingly and saying:

"Catkin, Catkin shining bright
in the forest of God's Light
there the humblest, kindest one
shines the most like the sun.
When the Light fills your heart strong
on your journey you'll speed along.
Your fur will be all sparkling clean
when you're never important and never mean."

The next morning she woke up almost cheerfully. After turning round and round, she sat on the ground, closed her eyes and saw a very bright Light. After looking at the inner Light for some time she felt a great peace within her. She found some cat mint and a little pool of clear water. After a delicious breakfast she started off.

As she walked along, further down
she met a sort of funny clown —
a cat, of sorts, but not like her —
a common cat with bright orange fur.

"Beautiful lady," said this cat.
"I don't have even a minute to chat,"
started Catkin to royally say,
but then remembered the different way.
"It's nice to meet you," she said instead,
and, smiling sweetly, she bobbed her head.
"If you're traveling to the Faery King,"
the orange cat said, all bright smiling,
"I can show you a good highway —
you'll go very fast today."
And Catkin knew in her heart,
she had made a lovely start.

And on it went. In every morning
her soul saw the inner Light dawning.
In each day's journey she found new ways
to grow in kindness by effort and grace.
She saw her most important task
was to smile sweetly at all and ask
of any she met upon her way,
'How are you this bright, fine day?'
"It is a sort of game this task.
My Lord is there behind each mask.

When I learn to honor and listen
his eyes are happy — they glow and glisten.
When I am patient a little while
I see him in each masked one's smile."

That day a raccoon, very pleased,
brought her a tasty garbage piece.
"It's very smelly," then said she,
and thought: 'not at all fit for me' —
but caught that thought just in time
and, smiling sweetly, oh-so-kind,
thought instead how she might please.
"I'd love to taste a little piece,"
she said, and ate a tiny part.
The purr she felt in her heart
told her she'd made another start.

"If you're traveling to the Faery King,"
the rough raccoon said, all bright smiling,
"I can show you a shorter way —
you'll go very fast today."

That night Catkin found a kindly cow who gave her some milk for dinner. After finishing every drop, she cleaned her whiskers and gave her paws a few licks before lying down to sleep. In the morning the inner Light shone as bright as the outer sun. She felt full of good cheer. "Maybe I'll cover a really good distance today," thought Catkin as she started walking.

Just then she saw coming near
a filthy rat with a crooked leer.
The ugliest thing she'd ever seen —
she only hoped he wasn't mean.
"Oh pretty kitty," said the rat,
politely tipping his old gray hat.

Catkin, smiling at the rat,
said, "Oh please, sir, stop and chat."
"I'd love to," said the scruffy, old thing
as his form did change — it was the King!

"Don't you know me, Catkin dear?"
And Catkin, suddenly seeing clear
saw a vision sweet and good,
where before the rat had stood.

"Oh if you're traveling to the Faery King,"
said he all bright shining,
"I will travel with you a way —
we'll go very fast today.

"Little Catkin," he continued on.
"Haven't you noticed your dirt is gone?
When you forgot how great you were

all the filth left your fur —
you've been quite sparkling clean
for a while now it seems."

And so, her trials mostly past
they traveled a good way very fast.

That night Catkin stopped to rest in a field of new-mown hay. She ate a lovely morsel of fresh farmer's cheese the Faery King had given her before they parted. When she bent to lap up some water from a crystal-clear pond at the side of the field, Catkin saw her reflection clearly in the water. "Why I'm all skin and bones," she thought, "and my fur has gotten gray and thin and fallen out around my ears. Could it be? Do I look old? Yes. It's awful but it's true — I look old and not very pretty any more." She turned to walk away and, to her horror, found that she was limping. "Why I think I hurt my leg when I hung from that hunter's snare. I've been concentrating so much on being kind to others that I hadn't even noticed.

"Oh, even if I do reach the Faery King, what will he think of me now? Will he accept me as old and ugly as I am?" she wondered. The rich scent of lush alfalfa hay surrounded her. Tired, she curled herself around and, thinking of her Faery King, fell asleep at last.

The next morning as she looked within herself, she seemed to float upward into golden Light even brighter than the outer sun. She felt so happy and cheerful afterwards that she forgot all about herself again and started out filled with yearning to reach the castle of her King.

And as it finally came to pass
she reached her Faery King at last.
To be with him was a gift she was given —
her pains fled as by an enchanter driven.

"Oh Catkin you are mine today!"
her Faery King exclaimed, "Hurray!"
And as he took her close to him,
they both turned their eyes within.

Her youth and beauty returned so bright,
it lit the countries of the night
with a brilliant golden Light
much brighter than the outer sun.
Now her journey — at last — was done.

For so long and long had she wandered. For so long and long had she walked. Then, when she reached him, all the ages fell away, as did her weariness of wandering. She rose above her cat form, and soul and Lord were one.

And where she'd passed the castle gate, at the edge of the garden, at the edge of the meadow, at the edge of the forest, flowers grew — tulips, daffodils and narcissus gave the sight and scent of joy, singing nature's song along with all the birds and beasts and every atom of creation to celebrate her new-found freedom. They sang to honor the little cat who'd walked across hundreds and thousands of miles for Love.

Secret Love

There was a girl
I'll tell you of
who discovered a secret—
the secret of Love.

Naomi Epstein was a medium–sized girl, sort of plain–looking, sort of quiet. She lived with her mom, dad and two brothers in a little town quite a distance into the country.

Naomi loved her family. She liked school and didn't mind her chores, but when those were done, what she liked best was to walk in the fields, in the woods, and along the roadsides where she lived.

She loved to see the colors of the trees, the meadows, the flowers, the butterflies, and the birds. She loved to watch the squirrels, the rabbits, the groundhogs and sometimes, when she was very lucky, the deer.

Because Naomi was a gentle girl and peaceful in her ways, often the animals would let her come quite close to them and she could watch them playing.

She loved all the seasons. She liked to see the colors and shapes changing. Most of all, though, she loved the summer. She loved to walk along the dirt roads, hearing the crunch of gravel and seeing the smooth–baked earth. She liked to watch the dust dancing in the breeze and smell the fragrance it gave off as it baked in the hot sunlight.

One day, full of happiness, and filled to the brim with the quiet joy of nature, she bent down, touched the dust she was walking upon and said, "I love you, dust."

To her great surprise, the dust replied," I love Him."

She went to a huge old maple tree along the road and hugged it saying, "You are so beautiful. I sit often in the cool shade you give. In autumn, I take your red, fallen leaves home as gifts to my mom and dad. I love you very much."

But the tree said,"I love Him."

Naomi was more surprised. She turned around and ran quickly to one of her favorite places — a place where rocks had pushed through the surface of the earth and stood like an island in a sea of grass and flowers. She hopped up and, finding her favorite seat upon the largest rock, shouted out to the surrounding meadow, "I love you!"

"We love Him," the meadow answered back, as a passing wind curved all the grasses and flowers into one dancing direction, as if bowing, all in unison.

Dear rocks, you have been here for me through sun, rain and snow. I love you," she said, patting the rock next to where she sat.

"We also love Him," they replied.

"And so do we," whispered the wind.

"As do we," said a chipmunk, accompanied by three of her young.

"And we," sang a chorus of golden finches.

"And we," piped up a chickadee–dee.

"I think I could speak for all of us?" asked a rather old robin looking at the many types of birds who had gathered round.

"Yes," they sang.

"We all love Him," said Robin.

A butterfly fluttered quite dancingly onto a flower growing near the rock island on which Naomi sat. "I love Him," the butterfly said sweetly.

A rabbit, running on the other side of the meadow, stood up on his rear paws. He looked at Naomi, wiggled his nose, and, lifting his front paws to his mouth, called out from that distance, "I also love Him."

"Do you all — earth, air, bird, beast, plant, flower, do you all love Him?" asked Naomi.

There was a sound in the air — the sound of a distant, drumming rumble, like gentle waves on a far-off shore or summer lightning thunder. It was a sound like humming, like many wings, or muted strings dancing in a delight of wonder, as if flowers had voices as pure as their iridescent, glowing, innocent hearts. The choir sang, "Yes — we all love Him, every one."

Naomi felt a joy, a delight, an excitement, and a tingling go through her as if she stood upon the brink of some far distant and barely dreamed of shore, as if she were about to find a door into a summer that might never end.

"Who is He?" she whispered.

It was partly a song, partly a dance; partly a kiss and a laughing glance. The sound she heard, and the colors around, sang of Paradise lost — but sometimes found....

He is the whole
of which each is part.
Of all, there are none
not part of His One.

He is the between,
the above and the under,
the joy of giving,
the life of wonder.

If you seek Him,
you start to know.
He loves us all,
whether high or low.

The peace of all beauty,
earth below, sky above,
lives in Him and is Him —
He is God — He is Love.

Sun, Moon & Stars

Native American Stories

Star Girl

(The concept of a star coming to earth and living as a woman is based on an Ojibway folk tale.)

nce there was a young star who lived in the Land of Peace, who looked down upon the earth and found it beautiful. Every night and every day she looked upon the earth and saw the beauty of its fields and trees and flowers and streams and the sweetness of the people and creatures who lived upon it. Gradually she fell in love with it all.

The desire to go to earth to live among its people and creatures and experience the wind and rain, heat and cold, day and night, became so strong that she went to Grandmother Moon and asked for permission to go.

"But Little Star," said Grandmother Moon, "You cannot go to earth as a star, for stars do not walk upon the earth. You would have to go as a person. If you become human, you will forget that you are really a star. You will be happy sometimes and sad sometimes. Life on earth is hard. There is pain, loneliness, illness and old age as well as joy and sweetness. Only if you could somehow remember your real self, would you be able to return to the Land of Peace."

"I understand, Grandmother," said Little Star. "Nevertheless, I long to live upon the earth."

"Very well," said Grandmother Moon. "I will send you and, because I love you, I will grant you a blessing. You may see the Light of the Land of Peace by looking within you. When you look upon that inner Light, you will feel joy and peace and that peace will stay with you."

Upon the earth, day followed night and night followed day. Summer followed spring. Spring followed winter and winter followed fall. All of nature and the people and creatures of the earth wove the patterns the Great Spirit had designed for them.

In the course of time, Strong Bow and Early Dawn of the Ojibway people married. Early Dawn had a vision that a noble soul would be sent to them as their child. Soon a beautiful baby girl was born to them. They named her Little Star because she was so merry and her eyes so bright.

As Little Star grew she was loved by her parents and her friends and she loved them as well. She was a happy child, but sometimes at night when she looked at the heavens, a homesickness crept into her heart. It was then she discovered if she closed her eyes but stayed awake and peaceful, she could see a beautiful Light shining in the darkness within her inner vision. When she looked into this Light she felt wonderfully cozy and contented as she drifted off to sleep.

With the passing of time Little Star grew into a woman. The time for marriage soon arrived. All the young men of the village called upon her and asked her parents for permission to marry her, for she had grown into a sweet young maiden as beautiful as she was good.

Her parents gave Little Star permission to choose her husband herself. She considered the matter for some time. Birch Bow was tall and strong. Bright Water was very handsome. Brown Elk was well–spoken as well as rich. And then there was Deep Water. He was very good-natured and skilled at hunting. He had an especially fine sense of humor. And what was most noticeable about him was that he was kind to every single person in their tribe. He talked nicely to young and old, poor and powerful alike. And everyone in the tribe knew that Deep Water was the one person who could be counted on for help no matter what the problem was. But he had fallen from a high rock as a child and, because of the fall, he walked with a limp and had scars on his face. Because he was the least handsome physically, the tribespeople felt he had no chance with Little Star who was very beautiful.

Little Star thought long and carefully, "Everyone I know feels unhappy some of the time. When I can ease someone's burden or make someone happier, I feel happier myself. All the young braves of our tribe are good, but Deep Water is the only one who feels the same way I do about helping people." So, thinking this, Little Star chose Deep Water and they were wed.

Deep Water was a loving husband. Both his parents and her own lived near them. Little Star's duties and her close-knit family life kept her busy and contented. In her happiness, she forgot her inner sadness. It just faded away...for awhile.

In due course, a daughter was born to Deep Water and Little Star. The baby, called Starbright, brought even more joy into Little Star's life. Still — sometimes — she felt there was something important she had forgotten. When she gazed at the starry sky at night she almost remembered, but no — it never really became clear.

There was always a lot of work to do. In fact, from the time the maple sap flowed in early spring through the ripening of the various berries in the summer and the crop plants in the fall, and then throughout the winter, there were duties from dawn to sundown. Life was busy and full, but Little Star still felt that something she couldn't quite place was missing. It seemed there was something else especially important she should be doing, but she couldn't remember what.

Still, Deep Water was as kind and caring as Little

Star had thought he would be. His love was her constant joy. He not only took care of their own family but spent his extra time in helping others. Little Star also helped any time and any way she could. Sometimes it was sharing food with those too ill to work in the fields, or tending someone sick, or sitting with someone grieving to cheer them. It was a good life — busy with work, worship, helping those in need, and the sharing of joyful affection and love with their family.

As time went by, however, sorrow came as regularly as joy. Her mother-in-law died suddenly. Then, just several months later, her father-in-law was killed in an accident. Their deaths left Little Star heartbroken, for she had come to love them both very much.

But next to her sorrow lived the joy Little Star received from her daughter, Starbright. By now, Starbright was a tall young girl, and the time spent in teaching her gave Little Star much pleasure as did the love she shared with Deep Water, a love which had grown stronger over all these years.

Time passed quickly. Soon Starbright was old enough to marry. She chose a good and loving young brave, and Little Star and Deep Water were pleased and joyful.

But then Early Dawn, her mother, died and Strong Bow, her father, became weak and was tired all the time. He was no longer able to care for himself, so Little Star cooked and cleaned for him. He had been so strong and so kind. Seeing him old and helpless grieved her terribly, but she carried out her duties as cheerfully as she could.

It was in the spring, when all the trees were budding with new leaves and new flowers peeped through the old fallen leaves on the forest floor, that her father's spirit finally passed from his body. Little Star had loved her father very much and his death brought deep pain to her heart.

After her father's death, one night as she closed her eyes to sleep, she saw the inner Light she had seen as a child and since forgotten. She decided that she would look at the inner Light every night before sleep because she found it so comforting.

But the necessities of daily life pulled Little Star's attention back into the many, many things she had to do and, once more, she forgot about the Light within her. Starbright had just given birth to a little girl and Deep Water and she found that helping with their granddaughter was one of the greatest joys they'd ever known.

But then, just one year after the birth of their grandchild, Deep Water fell ill and neither Little Star's care nor the shaman's medicines seemed to help. He became weaker with every passing day. One evening, as autumn winds shook the dry leaves from the trees, his spirit passed away from his body.

The next day all the tribe gathered to bury him and pay him honor. Little Star, her daughter, son-in-law, and granddaughter bade him farewell as his body was buried in the ritual customary to their tribe, so his soul could take the Path of Souls back to the Land of Peace, the Land of Love. For a time there was quiet. The mourners sat in a circle around the grave. Then, with the older men and women going first, the people of the tribe spoke. Almost every person there, adult and child alike, had a story to tell of Deep Water's virtue and the kindness he had shown them.

Little Star's grief was unbounded. The love she had shared with Deep Water had been the greatest joy of her life. She knew that one day their spirits would be reunited in the Land of Peace — that this was only a temporary separation, not a final parting — but still she missed him terribly.

The sympathy of her daughter and her tribe gave her consolation, but her greatest relief and comfort came from gazing long and deeply at the sweet, inner Light she once again remembered to look for within.

One day, feeling the need to walk in the woods and meadows, she walked to the village lake. As she looked into the water, she saw her reflection. Her hair, once black and glossy, was gray. Her face, once smooth and pretty, was wrinkled.

Next to her reflection she saw a water lily. As she looked out across the water, she saw hundreds of lilies floating upon it. As she looked, tears of grief filled her eyes. The lilies seemed to waver as her tears blurred her vision. The bright sun shone down upon the lake and all the lilies floating there. As she gazed upon this sight, it looked to Little Star as if each water lily was shimmering, dancing, and glittering like a many-colored rainbow of light. To her tear–filled eyes, the lilies appeared to be beautiful, shining stars.

All at once she remembered, "I am a star."

And, as she remembered, the Light within her flared up even more brilliantly than the sun, and Grandmother Moon came to her and stood beside her.

"Oh, Grandmother — you were right. With all the joys and all the sorrows, I forgot I was a star."

"But now you have remembered," said Grandmother Moon and she touched Little Star upon the forehead, whereupon her spirit flew out and went home.

So Grandmother Moon took Little Star home to the heavens, to the Land of Peace, the Land of Love, and there she was reunited with Deep Water, his parents Quarter Moon and Red Deer, and her parents Strong Bow and Early Dawn. It seemed as if the sorrow of their parting had been a dream dreamed long, long ago. Rose and lily petals rained from the skies and a beautiful light surrounded Little Star and her loved ones.

When the covering of the body is taken away and

the soul can be seen for what it truly is, each spirit
shines with a wonderful brilliance. When the truth is
known — everybody is a star.

Starsight

Neoka was an old woman who was much re-spected by her tribe. One day, she called her grandson to her side.

"Come here, boy. I am feeling old today. Soon my spirit will go to the Land of Peace. I am not afraid," she said and smiled. "I have had the good fortune to know more than many people are able to. I will go to a good place and will be at home there. I will be happier there than the greatest happiness I have ever known here.

"But before I go, I want to pass on what happened to me during a sacred vision-quest that I have kept secret for many years. I have watched you younger ones carefully, hoping to find someone I could share this with."

"And you have chosen me?" asked the boy.

"Yes," said the old woman. "All of you are good children. You do not lie or steal or hurt. But out of all of the children, you are special. I have seen you put a fallen baby bird back into its nest. I have seen you watching the wind and wishing you could fly as it does. Listen to my story, child. Listen well."

The old woman sat cross-legged on a rough wool

blanket. Her grandson sat before her. A meadow of wild asters, Queen Anne's lace and prairie grasses stretched from where they sat up to the far horizon in one direction and to the edge of the woods in the other. Neoka's eyes seemed to look inwards as she began to speak:

When I was a young girl, I was not exactly like the others. I was bold and wandered alone in the fields. I listened to the voice of the wind and the songs of the birds. I wanted to know my spirit as the ancient people of our tribe had. I wanted to find the truth hidden to open eyes. I wanted more than the world could give me. I longed to ride the wind and dance with the sun.

My father told me he was proud of me. My mother died when I was young and I tried my best to take care of my father and make our home warm with love for him. One day he told me he knew my heart's desires and he blessed me. He wished for me that my life would be bubbling with joy, like a brook bubbling downstream in the sun; he wished that my heart and words would be as sweet as a bird's song. He wished that my spirit would be as bright as a shining star. He gave me a nickname — Twinkling — like a young star's light. He told me I should stay true to myself so that my spirit would grow strong.

Then, one day, not long after my father's blessing, as I walked in a field in the northern part of our land, I saw a man standing before me. I wasn't afraid of him.

I could see that he was not an ordinary man because there was a golden light, very soft, around him. I thought perhaps he was a spirit–person and I waited, hoping he would speak to me.

"Twinkling, child of my heart," he said. This made me very happy. He was a spirit–person or how could he have known my nickname?

"Child," he said. "I have seen you in the fields. I have heard your dreaming. You are right. I am not of this time, of this earth. I live in the beautiful worlds within. I can travel here when I wish. I visit those whose hearts are pure, and I call to those who wish to come near."

"What is your name, spirit–person?" I asked.

"I have many names," he said. "I have as many names as there are peoples on the earth. Whoever lives by kindness and truth lives for me and whoever calls to goodness calls to me. You may call me Starsight for now. Later, if you wish, you may call me what you will. We will travel together and we will be friends."

"Where will we go, Starsight?" I asked.

"I will take you to the world beyond this one where Love is law. I will take you into the wind so that you may ride; and to the sun so that you may dance. If your dream is of goodness, and your heart is true, your dream may someday become real for you."

He touched me on the forehead. His eyes grew very large and looked as if diamonds were filling them. The golden light around him grew very bright and surrounded me also. Then, I saw a different world around me. People of all different races and colors were there. Their faces were soft and kind. They were happy. There was a many-colored light glowing softly all around. I felt so lighthearted, so peaceful. I knew it was the world within, the world where Love was law.

"Why isn't our world like this one, Starsight?" I asked.

"Because the hearts of the people of your world do not follow the Law of Love," he said. "On earth, too, Love is law, but many people have forgotten this while others have never learned. It is written: As you give, so shall you receive. Those who give love receive love; those who give pain receive pain. If you help others, you are helped; if you hurt others, you are hurt.

"Still, there is always hope. Each person has a soul. The soul, itself, is a seed of kindness that lives within everyone. In time, the seed grows stronger. Then, that person starts to turn away from other things and longs for love. When the longing grows strong enough, I come. I teach the Law of Love; it is always the same. If a person is ready, he or she hears me and lives by this law. Then the darkness leaves and that person is free from the fear and pain that most people live in."

"Starsight, may I stay here? I feel so at home," I asked.

"Each person on the earth has a time to live out there," he said. "But when your time on earth is through, I will come for you and bring you back here.

"Close your eyes. What do you see?" he asked.

"Golden sunlight — it's so beautiful," I replied.

"What do you hear?" he asked.

"Music. I can't describe it. It's more beautiful than anything I've ever heard," I said.

"Shall we dance with the sun? Hold tight and let me take you into the wind."

And he put his arms around me, lifted me and we were flying.

I saw all the earth, its oceans, its mountains, its forests. He took me close. I saw its people. He touched my eyes. I saw their many faces — some yellow, some tan, some brown, some very dark, some very pale. Everywhere I saw that life was the same. Each person was born and would die. Each baby needed love, care, food and shelter. Each person grew up and needed to work, to survive, to understand life's mysteries and to be fulfilled by living in harmony with them. Each person felt sometimes afraid or sad or lonely; sometimes happy or full of joy. Each person needed love. I saw the poor ones, the rich ones, the kind ones, the mean ones. I saw caring actions, but I also saw cold, cruel actions as people ignored the pain of others. Finally our journey was over.

We had flown around the world following the

turning of the sun, but when we returned to my father's field the shadows fell as they had before we started. "Has any time passed by, Starsight?" I asked.

"There are laws beyond time," he told me, smiling. We rested then, sitting down amidst the flowers and grasses. My heart was happy but also sad when I remembered the many unhappy things I had seen among the earth's people.

"Starsight, what is wrong with this world?" I asked. "Everywhere I saw so many people treat each other so badly. Why does that happen?"

"When people put money, power, and possessions first, usually they do not care to help others. Instead, they are thinking all the time of the things they desire. They hurt others on purpose or through ignorance and in return they are hurt. They have forgotten being kind and the joy it gives. As you give, so you receive — this is nature's law. It is very sad."

"Starsight, can I help?"

"Yes, little Twinkling. I will tell you how. As you live out your life, you live by the Law of Love. If someone is sad, try to cheer him. If someone is hungry, try to feed him. If someone is in need, try to help him. Do your best. You will feel peace and know joy because you will be living for love and for me. If others see your joy, your peace, they will ask you about it. You can help them find the strength, the hope to dream. If they can dream of love, they also will find me."

"But, Starsight, what of the world?"

"As more hearts grow, as more spirits waken, the world also will change. Some day the Law of Love will rule and the suffering will end. Then, all the earth will dance."

"Starsight, may I be with you again?" I asked.

"When you have time, sit quietly and think of me," he said. "Remember our time today together. Call to me in your heart. Close your eyes for awhile. If your mind can be still, I will come to you; and remember, I will always be watching over you. You are very dear to me. I won't forget you."

And then he was gone and I was in the northern field again, alone.

"I sang a song then in my heart, boy. I have tried to live that song. I know where I'm going and now I want to give my song to you...."

I walked one day with Starsight,
We flew within the wind.
He taught me the ways of love's Light —
I pray I'll not forget him.

Where do our heart's dreams come from?
From where do good dreams come?
Who can give a soul's unfolding
And dancing with the sun?

Oh, life is full of crying,
So many ways of pain,
But if a soul can find Him,
Then rainbows light the rain.

Oh, may I live by Love's law
and may my heart be true.
And may I stay in Love's Light —
Starsight, ever, with you.

The sun was setting behind the trees. A coral and lavender glow lined the horizon. Neoka stood up and reached for her grandson's hand. "Time to go back, boy," she said.

The young boy held the old woman's rough, work-worn hand in his. "Can I have a sacred vision also, Grandmother?" he asked.

"If your heart is true and you seek it, you will find it," Neoka replied.

"I will never forget, Grandmother," he said. "I will live the truth as you have."

Hand in hand they walked towards the red, setting sun and home.

Back from the Stars

My great, great grandmother was named Little Star. My family's tradition says she was sent to earth to live as a human being so that she could show our people what a shining-bright life would be.

My grandmother was named Neoka, but her secret name was Twinkling. She told me so herself. When I was very young my grandmother called me aside and told me of her childhood and her great adventure with the spirit-person, Starsight. I have never forgotten what she told me. It went from her heart to mine. I have tried to live by the Law of Love as Starsight told her and she told me.

When my family could no longer earn a living on our tribal land, we moved to a small town where my dad was able to get a job. It's harder to live by the Law of Love here than it was in the country, but I've kept on trying. I always believed giving love and living by the Law of Love were the most important things on earth. Now I know it.

When I first moved here, Hal, the biggest boy in my class and a real bully, started calling me names.

"Hey, injun, you weirdo-freak!" he would say and laugh. My skin color is dark reddish-looking just as my ancestors' skin was. I wear my hair pretty long and tied back, so I look different from most of the other kids, but I never thought it would be so difficult to fit in.

Maybe in a big city it would have been easier. In this town, though, most of the families have lived here for a long time and they are all white. I think many of the kids would have accepted me if it hadn't been for Hal. He seemed to think my reddish skin and long, black hair meant I was evil. How could the way the Creator made a person look be evil? But Hal would chant "The only good injun's a dead injun," and threaten to come and beat me up. I'm used to taking care of my own problems, so I thought if I treated him and his friends with tolerance and respect they would finally realize that I was just another person.

But it didn't work out like that. The more tolerant I was, the more bitter Hal got. He seemed to enjoy hating someone, and I was the one he picked out to hate. Last winter, as I was walking home from school, Hal and two boys from his gang attacked me. I didn't want to fight. I didn't want to hurt anyone. One of the boys, Jim, tried to stop the other two, but they wouldn't listen. Hal started calling me names and hitting me. I tried to get away and ran across the street. There was a loud noise and I felt a big explosion knock me over.

Then I found myself above my body. I was looking

down on the street. My body was lying beside a car. There was a siren and the police came roaring up. One of the policemen was talking to the driver and the other was kneeling beside my body. Jim was still there, crying. The other two boys were gone.

The next thing I knew, I floated up toward the sky. Then, the sky got darker and I was zooming through a tunnel. Wind rushed past me. I was flying towards a circle of bright light at the end of the tunnel. Suddenly I found myself on the shore of a big lake. There were all kinds of beautiful trees and flowers there. The colors of everything were shining and glowing.

"Waubun-anung, it is good you are here," said a being made of brilliant golden light.

"But where is here?" I asked. "Who are you and how do you know the ancient form of my name?"

The being made of light became a beautiful man with the kindest face I've ever seen. He said "Morning Star" (for that is the meaning of Waubun-anung) "your family is dear to Kitche Manitou, the Great Spirit. In ancient days, boys of twelve years and older were thought old enough to seek a vision-quest. Life without inner vision was considered shallow and meaningless."

Just then there was another shimmer of golden light and two women appeared standing on either side of the beautiful man I first saw.

"I am Starsight," said the man.

"And I am Little Star," said one of the women.

"And I am your grandmother, Neoka," said the other woman. "Don't you remember me?"

"But you look so young, Grandmother, and you are glowing," I said.

"Here our souls take the shapes that our thoughts, words and deeds have created in life," my grandmother replied, as she came close and hugged me.

"But what am I doing here? What is this place?" I asked.

"This is the Land of Love, and you are here to meet your spirit-guide," replied Neoka.

"But who is my spirit-guide and why do I need one?" I asked.

"I am your spirit-guide, my Morning Star," replied Starsight.

"Am I dead?" I asked.

"Your soul has traveled from your body," said Starsight, "but you are still connected to it by a silver cord. You are here to visit a while and learn, but then you must return."

"Learn what?" I asked.

"It is time for you to learn more of the mystery behind the life you see on earth," said Little Star. "When you are in your earth body, it is hard to know that you are really a soul wearing a body as, on earth, you wear clothing."

"But what is this mystery of which you speak, and why have I been chosen to learn it?" I asked.

"There are laws that govern everything in the universe," said Starsight. "On earth many people have forgotten, but those laws still control the destiny of all lives. Those laws and their effects form the great mystery of life that each soul must unravel.

"Long ago, the Great Spirit, Kitche Manitou, created the earth and all the plants, creatures and human beings upon it. Everything was in its place and everything was beautiful. For a time all was in harmony as He had formed it. Then, certain beings longed for power of their own. With that desire and the actions that followed, strife and discord came onto the earth. No longer did all the plants, animals, and humankind understand each other's language. No longer did they live in peace, nourished by the sustenance their spirits drew from air, sunshine, and water.

"The Great Spirit was sad to see the pain and misery that hatred and violence brought to His creation. He sent a vision to great souls among the humankind — a vision of life lived in harmony, peace, and love for one another. To this very day when a soul is ready to learn the higher way — the Law of Love — that soul is brought closer to learn."

"But what am I to see? What am I to learn?" I asked.

Starsight came close to me. He smiled and his face glowed with beautiful, soft, bright light. "Only the bravest and the strongest can forgive and love, my Morning Star," he said. "Remember that."

All of a sudden, I was on a high hill. I was able to look down at the earth as if through a circle of glass. I saw Jim and Hal and the other boy who had attacked me. But I didn't just see them, I also felt their feelings and heard their thoughts. They were full of fear and anguish. Jim felt ashamed of what had happened, but Hal and the other boy felt only fear and hatred. Their spirits were surrounded by dark clouds of writhing, gray smoke and dim, eerie flames.

"If you give hatred, you are hated," said Neoka. "Worst of all, you hate yourself and thus your spirit can never be at peace."

Then, with a sound of rushing waters, I found myself on a small island, surrounded by deep ocean waters. I saw a boat had crashed there and three people were marooned. One was white, one was brown, and one was black.

One man's legs were injured but his arms were whole and strong. One man's arms were injured but his legs were whole and strong. One man had injured both his arms and his legs but his face was clear and wore a bright, intelligent expression.

It was obvious to me that none of the three people could see me, though I could see them clearly. As I watched, the man with the bright face told the other two how to fix the boat and make oars. The man with strong arms pulled the broken boat towards him and started mending it with vines and sap. Then he took a sharp rock and shaped driftwood into oars which he put into the boat. He tied the boat with vines around the waist of the man with strong legs and that man walked to the water, dragging the boat behind him. Walking into the water until the boat was mostly in the water but still just a bit on the shore, he shook the vines off leaving the boat at the water's edge.

The man with strong arms picked up the bright-faced man with one arm and, with the other arm, held onto the man with strong legs who carried both the others down to the boat where he lowered the other two over the sides before getting in himself.

The man with strong arms prepared to start rowing. All of a sudden, the waves stopped tossing, the sun came out and a sound like beautiful church bells filled the air.

"If you help others, you will be helped," said Little Star.

"Only through harmony and cooperation can any person (and the entire world) survive," said Neoka.

Then, I felt myself swirling through the air. I landed in a cave. It was pitch black inside. I could hardly breathe.

"Where am I?" I called. "What is this about?"

All of a sudden I saw the darkness was lighter towards one side of me. I walked in that direction. As I walked, it became lighter and lighter. As I came to the wall of the cave, I saw there was an opening above me. I climbed up and up, finally reaching the top of the cave which opened out onto a high plateau.

I climbed out and, to my amazement, I saw that Hal was standing on the plateau right next to its overhanging edge. As I watched, he slipped and fell. He was dangling in the air, hanging on by one hand to a small shrub growing near the edge of the precipice.

I ran over to him. He looked up from where he was hanging and saw me.

"Save me, Morry, save me," cried Hal.

I didn't think Hal even knew my name. He had sure never used it before. It was always, "Hey, injun boy," or worse. I started to pull him up, but I couldn't forget the hours and days of abuse and torment Hal had put me through. My mind felt like it was on fire when I remembered how this very person had attacked me and left me wounded — possibly dying — in the street.

"No!" I shouted, "I won't help you. Not you!" But as I said it, I remembered the love my mother and father had given me. I remembered their teaching that forgiveness was one of God's most beautiful gifts. I remembered Starsight's sweet, loving, face as he whispered, "Be strong and full of courage, my Morning Star, only the strongest and most brave can forgive."

I stood frozen. I didn't want to forgive Hal. I wanted him to get the punishment he deserved. I started to turn away and let him fall to the rocks below but, as I did, I thought I heard Starsight's sweet voice saying, "Where there is forgiveness, there the Great Spirit rejoices. Where there is mercy, there is peace and joy. Only the strongest and most brave can forgive...."

I had to be strong — I had to do it. How could I look Starsight in the eyes again if I failed?

"I will forgive you!" I shouted. I ran to the other boy's side. "I still don't like you, but I believe in love more than anything else in the whole world so I will help you!" Then I took hold of Hal's hand and pulled him up, back from the precipice and onto the land at the edge of the plateau.

There, to my great surprise, Hal's form shimmered, changing into that of Starsight.

"You have learned enough for today, my son," he said.

Then we traveled, as if on a magic carpet of clouds, through the air until we were back on the beautiful shores of the peaceful lake with the glorious scent of blossoms surrounding us and the sweet music of a soulful flute playing gently through the air. Neoka and Little Star were there, hand in hand, smiling.

"It is time for you to return, Waubun-anung, my Morning Star," said Starsight.

And when he said that, I remembered my mother and father. I knew they would be missing me, and I knew that it was true; it was time for me to return.

"It's so beautiful here," I said. "Will I be able to come back here?"

"It is possible, my Morning Star. You will have to learn to still your mind in meditation for this to happen. You will have to look within for the true vision. If you can see the Light of the Great Spirit within you, your soul will be able to return, although your body will stay on earth just as it has today."

"But how can I learn to see it?" I asked.

"Teacher-souls were promised to humankind by the Great Spirit," Starsight replied. "In fact, one of the great teachers of your people, Deganawidah, taught The Great Peace among the Iroquois and other tribes.* If you want to learn, the way will open.

"But know this my child—even if you do not return until your soul leaves your body at the time your stay on earth is through, you can still live by the Law of Love and thus bring much happiness to yourself and those around you.

"Be loving, forgiving and kind. Help anybody who needs help however you can. Be truthful. Look on everybody as your family, the family of the Great Spirit, and trust in His Love for you.

"If you live this way, you will be happy and at peace. As your life touches others, you will help bring the Law of Love to earth. Each person can only change himself or herself, but when many have changed, the circle will come full round and a golden age will come to pass."

Neoka, Little Star and my now-beloved Starsight gathered around me. Their faces were full of peace. I could feel their hearts full of love for all beings and, especially it seemed, love for me. I threw my arms around Starsight. We hugged each other tightly.

I felt such joy, such happiness. It's hard to explain it, but it stayed in my heart as we said good-bye.

Then I was traveling back through the sort of swirling tunnel I had passed through at the very beginning of this adventure.

As I traveled I heard the voices of many of the tribespeople down through time chanting. I could understand what they said, although I had never learned any of the different languages I was hearing.

There is power in nature,
but what Power created nature?
What Power?
What Power created life?
What Power gave us bodies
in which to live?

What Power?
What Power put the sun, moon and stars
into the heavens?
And what Power keeps them from falling?
What Power?
What Power gave to earth her beauty?
The seasons in their glory,
and diversity of creation?
What Power?
What Power gave to all creation
these many gifts that we enjoy
before we pass away?
What Power?
What Power made the Path of Spirit?
What Power leads our way upon it
through earth life
to the Land of Love?
What Power?

I opened my eyes. I was lying in a white bed in a white room. There was a tube attached to my wrist leading to a bag hanging above and to the left of me. As I looked around I saw my mother and father and, as I saw them, they saw me. Their eyes lit up.

"Morry," my mother cried, "You've been unconscious for three days!"

"I knew you weren't gone forever," my father said. "I knew your spirit would return."

"The boy, Jim, told us what happened, Morry," my mother said.

"His parents went to the school board," my father said. "They begged the board to start nonviolent conflict resolution classes and other peace programs throughout the entire school."

"Jim told us it was Hal's idea to chase you," said my mother, "and even though Hal refused to admit it and acted as if he was happy you were hurt, his mother and father told us that they were ashamed of what he'd done and horrified that he'd gotten others to help him. They're going to pay for a lot of the peace materials themselves until an emergency tax levy can be passed."

"The whole community came forward to offer help," said my father.

"And everyone is glad about the new peace training," said my mother.

"Except maybe Hal," said my father.

"Even Hal has a heart," I said. "And when I get out of here I'm going to tell him some of the things that happened to me and some of the things I learned. I bet even Hal will find it pretty interesting."

"We love you so much," said my mom.

"Getting a peace program into our schools is a wonderful thing," said my dad. "Though I don't know if it was worth your getting hurt."

"Everything happens for some good reason," I

said. "The Great Spirit is watching over us all."

"Great Spirit?" said my mom in surprise.

"What, exactly, did happen to you while you were lying there unconscious?" asked my dad.

"It's sort of a long story," I said and, as I took a deep breath to begin the telling of it, I saw a soft golden glow fill the room and felt again the peace and joy of the Land of Love within my heart.

*Deganawidah taught The Great Peace among the Iroquois and other tribes about 1,459 A.D. He traveled widely, accompanied by Hiawatha, and taught that mental, physical and spiritual health would lead to continuing peace on earth.

Holly, Hearth & Home

Holiday Stories

Hanukkah Light

t was the eighth and last day of Hanukkah. Joshua had spun the dreidel or square top and received his gelt or gold-wrapped chocolate coins. Now he and his mom and dad would light the last of the eight candles in the menorah or nine-branched candelabrum with the shammus candle, a ninth candle used to light the other eight. After lighting the candles, Josh and his family would recite prayers and offer gratitude to God for the miracle of the lights. Long ago, when the Temple had been regained and was being sanctified for Jewish holy worship, there had only been oil enough to burn in the lamps for one day. Then, God had caused a miracle and, instead, the oil had burned for eight days.

Now Josh and his family would enjoy a festive meal featuring potato pancakes or latkes as was traditional. Josh and his family were vegetarians so their main course was meatless sauerbraten or cutlets in gravy. In addition to that they had tzimmes, a dish made of white potatoes, sweet potatoes and prunes, noodle kugel, a pudding-like casserole and, for dessert, egg-free macaroons and fried plum-cake donuts.

Abe, Josh's dad, passed the serving plate of latkes around the table. Rachel, Josh's mom, offered them sour cream and applesauce to put on top.

"Josh, I can take you to the store tomorrow to buy those new ice skates you wanted," said Abe.

"You got a lot of Hanukkah money this year," said Rachel. "You should be able to buy them easily."

"I took a look at those skates just last week. They're really great skates. I'd love to have them, but I'm not going to get them now," said Josh. "I'm going to get something else with the money instead."

"But Josh, you've been talking about those skates for weeks," said Abe. "You said they were racing skates and you needed them because you couldn't keep up with the other boys on your old kids' skates."

"I know, Dad," said Josh. "But now I want something else."

"Honestly, Josh," said Rachel. "You've been pestering us for racing skates, ever since the pond froze over. Those skates were all you could talk about. What else could you want to buy more than them?"

"I was over at the pond today, Mom," said Josh. "A bunch of us guys had been skating and then we got into a snowball fight. One of the kids, Tommie, always wears these real old skates that are all taped together. Today I saw he didn't have any gloves. He was making snowballs with his bare hands. Then I saw that the snow he was packing together had red stuff on it.

"After the snowball fight, I walked home with him. I started talking to him and I found out his dad is gone, and his mom works two jobs to support them. He doesn't have any gloves because the ones he had last year are way too small for him now. His hands were all chapped from the cold and bleeding. That red stuff on the snow was blood. So I want to spend my Hanukkah money to buy gloves for him. And if I have enough I want to get new skates for him too. My skates are old but they're safe. His are just taped together and if they broke he could hurt himself."

"Why, Josh, that's wonderful!" said Rachel.

"You know, Hanukkah is a festival of rededication to God and it was often thought to be a time to help others less fortunate than yourself," said Abe. "I'm really proud of you, Josh."

"I've got a date with Tommie for tomorrow," said Josh. "He thinks we're going skating, but I plan to take him to the store first."

"The real Hanukkah light is the joy we get from helping others," said Rachel. "I'm going to get to know Tommie's mom better. Maybe there's something more we can do to help."

The Hanukkah candles brightened the room with a soft glow. Josh and his mom and dad looked at each other and smiled.

An Attitude of Gratitude

Merlin Mouse had just moved out to the suburbs from the city. His mom and dad, Millie and Morton Mouse, had met and married while living at the University of Chicago and that's where Merlin was born and spent his early childhood. But, as Merlin got older, Millie and Morton thought the suburbs would be a better place for him to grow up, so they moved out to a cozy hole-in-the-wall in a two-car garage attached to a home on a nice lot with grass and trees.

It was the week before Thanksgiving when Merlin's family finally finished unpacking and settled in for good. Merlin missed his old playmates. He felt sad and grumpy.

One day as he sat on a brick next to the driveway he felt so lonely he started to cry. Just then an older mouse with gray fur and a kind smile came up to him and said, "Hey, what's wrong? Is there anything I can do?"

"Who are you?" asked Merlin, choking back his tears.

"I'm Reverend Bradley Mouse. I'm the preacher

for the mice community at All United Church," said Reverend Mouse. "Who are you?"

"My name's Merlin," replied Merlin.

"You look pretty sad, Merlin," said Bradley Mouse. "What's the matter?"

"We just moved here and I hate it. I'm really lonely. There are no mice kids to play with. I'm so bored I could scream. Then, to top it off, in a few days it'll be Thanksgiving. We aren't going anywhere. We don't know anyone here. Thanksgiving — ha, ha ha! That's a joke. I feel really rotten. It's Thanksgiving, but what do I have to be thankful for?"

"There's always something to be thankful for," said Bradley Mouse. "Listen, come to the church for Thanksgiving. We're going to have a community dinner that's open to all. You and your family will be more than welcome. It's that little brick church building on the corner of Elm and Sycamore. A lot of mice and mice kids will be there. You and your mom and dad can meet some nice mice there and have a wonderful dinner, too."

"Maybe we'll come. I'll ask Mom and Dad," said Merlin. "But that's not enough to make me feel thankful — sorry."

"Look here, Merlin," said Bradley Mouse. "I hate to see you feeling so unhappy. You could feel a lot better if you would just change your attitude and try to look at things a little differently. No matter how bad things may seem to us, there's always something to feel grateful for. If you try to see things that way, after awhile, you will and you'll find you feel a lot better when you do. We have to keep our minds open and try extra hard to see things with an attitude of gratitude. If we keep saying, 'Everything's horrible, everything's terrible,' then sure enough it will be."

"What do you mean?" asked Merlin.

"It's a different way of seeing the world. In this world there will always be things we like and things we don't like, things that make us happy and things that make us sad. If we learn to look for the things we like, the things that make us happy, then — after awhile, our mind will be filled with thoughts of happy things." Bradley Mouse cleared his throat and recited:

I feel sad
but it won't be so bad
if I see one thing
that makes me feel glad.

"Try it Merlin," he said. "And each day, you'll find more to be thankful for than you did the day before. Just give it a whirl and tell me what you think at Thanksgiving." And the old mouse smiled and walked away saying:

I want to lose this sad, bad mood

and get an
attitude of gratitude!

"Is that guy nuts or what?" said Merlin to himself, and moped around the yard kicking at the grass till he had kicked several places bare.

Next day Merlin woke up in a really bad mood. He felt so bad, so sad, and so mad he could hardly stand himself. "I've got to try something," he thought. "Okay, I'll do what the old guy said. Nothing could be worse than the way I feel now."

That day he looked everywhere to find just one thing that made him feel glad. And he found one! He realized how much he liked his mom and dad. The next day he realized how much he liked his mom's cooking, and the day after that he realized he liked the grass better than the concrete sidewalks where he used to live. Because he was counting things so he could be grateful for them, he noticed how many different things he had found in just three days. He also realized how much better he was feeling. Then he made friends with three little mice kids he met at the vacant lot down the street, which made him feel really glad!

On Thanksgiving morning he woke up feeling positively great. "Hey! I feel great!" he thought and then felt grateful for feeling so happy. "I guess I should be grateful for feeling grateful, too," he thought and laughed.

At about 2:00 p.m. Merlin, Millie and Morton walked over to the church at Elm and Sycamore. There Merlin saw his three new friends. He said hi and they all smiled at each other. He introduced them to Millie and Morton, and the mice kids introduced him to their parents. After the introductions were finished, they all walked up the sidewalk to the tiny church-mice door together.

There Bradley Mouse took Merlin aside. "How are you doing?" he asked.

"It really works!" said Merlin, "I feel great!"

Bradley Mouse smiled and patted Merlin on the head. Then, he cleared his throat (as was his habit) and recited:

> *Give thanks for what's good*
> *and if you do,*
> *more that's good*
> *will come to you.*
>
> *Think of thanks*
> *and you'll feel glad.*
> *Have no thanks*
> *and you'll feed bad.*
>
> *Give thanks for what's good*
> *and if you do,*
> *more that's good*
> *will come to you.*

Everyone clapped loudly. Reverend Bradley Mouse smiled and invited everyone in to give thanks to God for His bounty and join in the wonderful feast. 🐾

Merlin Mouse's Merry Christmas

erlin Mouse lived with his mom and dad in a small hole-in-the-wall in a two-car garage attached to a house in a quiet suburb outside Chicago.

Merlin's mom and dad, Millie and Morton Mouse, had met and married while living in the social science building at the University of Chicago. Then Merlin came along and, as Merlin got older, Millie and Morton decided to move out to the suburbs so Merlin could play in green fields instead of city streets.

Merlin had been lonely at first but now he loved his new home. He loved having a room of his own. He loved having a lawn outside with grass to play on. He loved the way the new house smelled. It didn't smell all bookish and musty like the social science building had, but instead, because their hole-in-the-wall was right behind the kitchen, it smelled like the chocolate chip cookies which Billy's mom often baked. Billy was the little boy who also lived in Merlin's new home.

What Merlin especially loved, however, was running through the walls and creeping out from a small opening in the wall next to the heat register in Billy's bedroom when Billy's mom was reading him stories at night. There Merlin could listen to all sorts of stories about all kinds of things he had never heard of before. As it happened, it was Christmas time, and Merlin thought the stories about Christmas trees and presents and Santa Claus were the most wonderful stories of all.

Soon Merlin told his mom and dad that he was going to be very good and make a wish list for Santa so Santa would know what to bring for him as well as for Billy. "I really, really want a red, toy truck," he said excitedly.

This was very upsetting to Millie and Morton. They knew that parents often acted as Santa's helpers during the Christmas rush but they also knew that they had no time to look for much at all, let alone a red toy truck. Merlin would be so disappointed. "It's the day before Christmas, Merlin. I'm afraid it's just too late," Millie said.

"But Mom," said Merlin, "Billy made a list. I saw him. Why can't I?"

"But his mom must have mailed it by now. Your letter can't possibly reach the North Pole by tonight. It's really too late for you," said Millie, not knowing what else to say.

"Then I'll pray to God. I heard it in the other stories Billy's mom reads. I listened really carefully because it sounded so wonderful. Billy's mom definitely said that God is there for all creation. She said God is there for everyone. He loves every leaf, bird, creature and person the same. If you're in trouble you can call to Him. He hears the cry of an ant before the trumpet of an elephant if the ant really needs Him. And if what you pray for is good for you, He'll answer your prayers."

"I don't know, Merlin," said Millie. "A red toy truck? By tomorrow?"

"I listened really carefully, Mom," said Merlin. Where all efforts fail, there prayer succeeds. It's highest to pray for whatever God thinks is best and next highest to pray for spiritual knowledge. But if you're young you can pray for something you really want if it doesn't hurt anybody else. That's what Billy's mom said. I heard her. Sometimes God knows that what you want wouldn't be good for you. Sometimes, since He knows everything, He knows that something else would be better. But if it's a cry of the heart, and it won't hurt you, He will answer your prayers."

That night, as Merlin lay in bed before going to sleep he thought, "My heart feels so happy when I hear about God. I know that means He is there for me. I can pray to Him (anybody anywhere can) and if it is a cry of my heart, He will hear me." So Merlin folded his paws together and prayed:

"Dear God, the story said you love us all, great and small, and hear the littlest heart's true call. If this is true, please, will you tell Santa Claus to bring me a present as well as Billy?"

That night Merlin dreamed that God came to him. Naturally, since it was Merlin who was dreaming, God looked like a very wise and loving mouse with white, shiny fur and sparkling bright eyes. God spoke to him in the kindest, most loving way and said:

> *He loves us all,*
> *great and small,*
> *and hears the littlest*
> *heart's true call.*
> *Just give it a try*
> *and make a start.*
> *He's always as close*
> *as the cry of your heart.*
> *So never give up*
> *and never despair,*
> *where all is lost, God is there.*
> *Call Him in need;*
> *if your cry is true,*
> *He will always be there for you.*

Meanwhile, earlier that afternoon, Merlin's father, Morton, had seen Billy throwing something away. He ran over after Billy was gone. When he looked he saw it was a red truck from Billy's miniature car and truck collection. It had a lot of nicks and scratches, but it still looked pretty good. Now there was real hope!

Morton ran to find some string. He found a piece of knitting yarn and tied it to the toy truck's steering wheel. Then, he dragged the truck as fast as he could to Millie, huffing and puffing just a little as he went along. "Millie, Millie," he wheezed (stopping to take a deep breath before continuing), "I've found a truck. Look, it's perfect, isn't it?"

Millie was so happy she squeaked! "Oh, yes, it *is* perfect, Mortie," she said. "And just this morning Billy's mom threw some bottles of old nail polish away. Maybe there's a red one — let me go see." She ran excitedly to look.

Morton went to see if he could find any scraps of thrown-away wrapping paper and, to his great delight, he did. Then, Millie came running up with a bottle of

nail polish that was exactly the right color. Morton gripped the bottle in his front paws while Millie unscrewed the cap with her strong teeth. They decided that Morton should fix the truck's paint and Millie would go look for a piece of evergreen bough to use for a tree.

The next morning was Christmas. Merlin got up very early and woke up Morton and Millie. They all went into the living room of their hole-in-the wall. There Millie and Morton had set up a small piece of the spruce tree Billy's mom and dad had set up in their living room. The little piece of tree was stuck into an old silver candle holder Morton had found in the trash. The little tree was decorated with cast-off bits of ribbon, old earrings, buttons, and shiny, sparkly pieces of aluminum foil gnawed and twisted into decorative shapes.

Merlin gave Millie and Morton a piece of cheese wrapped in red paper. They gave him a beautifully wrapped package with a big note saying "From Santa" on it. He unwrapped it and found, to his great delight, a red toy truck just his size! He couldn't believe his eyes. He was so happy, he jumped up and down for joy. They all hugged each other and Merlin gave each of his parents a big kiss.

"I guess God heard me," Merlin said delightedly.

"Who knows how miracles happen?" said Morton, thoughtfully.

"Where love is, God is there too," said Millie.

"Then God bless us all, every one!" said Merlin.

Millie brought out three bowls of Cheerios cereal and cream. She had recently found a toy set of dishes and cutlery just the right size for them. Merlin pushed his new truck over and sat down happily beside it. They thanked God for His love and kindness and then enjoyed their Christmas breakfast together. 🍃

Merlin Mouse's Merry Christmas 2

ast year Merlin and his mom and dad, Millie and Morton, had moved out from the city to the suburbs so Merlin could play in grassy fields instead of city streets.

It had been a great year for Merlin full of learning and doing wonderful, new things. Now it was Christmas time again and Merlin was really looking forward to Christmas day.

One day Merlin was playing outdoors in the snow. He was bundled up well, with a thick hat, gloves, a big muffler, and a warm coat and boots. His mom always told him it was very important to bundle up at all times when going out into the cold. There had been a big blizzard and the ground was covered with snow almost two feet high except where the humans had plowed and shoveled the streets, driveways and sidewalks. On each side of the cleared-off places huge mounds of snow rose up, some of them five to six feet high. For Merlin, this was very exciting — it was like a trip to the Alps or the Himalayas.

He had a shiny piece of tin he had found in the furnace room of his house and he was using it as a sled. He would climb up to the top of a big snow pile and then slide down in a glorious rush. He had found a new location towards the back of the yard of his house by the old wooden fence and rubbish bins with a wonderfully high pile of snow that had been cleared off the driveway. He had just climbed up to the top of the snow when he heard a small voice say "Hey, what are you doing?"

He looked around and saw, over by the rubbish bins, a little mouse about his size standing there shivering.

"Hi, I'm Merlin," Merlin shouted from the top of the snow pile. "Who're you?"

"I'm Matthew," the poor, cold-looking little mouse said.

"But why aren't you dressed right for this cold weather?" Merlin asked.

"My mom and dad and I just moved out here from the south and they haven't been able to find jobs yet," Matthew said. "We found a little hole-in-the-fence for a home but it's very cold and we don't have the right clothes for this weather."

Merlin thought really carefully. He knew that his mom and dad always liked to help other mice when they could and told him that was the right thing to do. Was there any way he could help Matthew? He remembered that his mom hadn't given away his winter clothes from last year yet and it looked like

Matthew was smaller than he was, so he said, "Matthew, wait here for a couple of minutes. I have an idea of something that might help. I'll be right back."

Merlin ran quickly back to his home, and told his mom what was wrong. She thought giving the winter clothes he had outgrown to Matthew was a wonderful idea and added some older sweaters, coats and boots that she and Morton didn't need as well. "And Merlin, why don't you invite Matthew and his parents over for Christmas tomorrow?" Millie said.

Merlin ran happily back to where Matthew was waiting. "Matthew, here are some clothes for you and maybe for your mom and dad, if they fit," Merlin said excitedly. "Take them and try them on. If they fit, keep them. And my mom wants you and your folks to come over tomorrow to our home to celebrate Christmas with us. Do you think you can?"

"These clothes look so nice, Merlin." Matthew said. "Thank you so much. I'm sure some of them will fit and it will be so wonderful to have something warm to wear. We aren't doing anything at all tomorrow, so I know Mom and Dad will want to go over to your house to celebrate Christmas with you. But, Merlin, will Santa bring you presents?"

Last year Merlin had found out that God would listen to the prayers of anyone and he had prayed and God had talked to Santa for him. This year he thought Santa would bring something but he wasn't entirely sure. "I don't know for sure, Matthew, why?" he asked.

"I only heard about Santa when we moved here," said Matthew. "I know Mom and Dad don't have any money at all and I don't either so I can't get them any presents. If only I could talk to Santa, then maybe he could bring something for my mom and dad. And, maybe, if he had room in his bag, he could bring something for me too."

"I don't know about talking to Santa," Merlin said. "It's really late now. It's the day before Christmas already, but I heard in the stories that Billy's mom reads that God is there for all creation. If you're in trouble you can call to Him. He loves every leaf, bird, creature and person the same. He hears the cry of an ant before the trumpet of an elephant if the ant really needs Him. And if what you pray for is good for you, He'll answer your prayers. Sometimes what you pray for might not be good for you or someone else — for some reason something else would be better — then you won't get what you pray for, because God always knows what's best, but if your prayer is good and it's a cry of your heart, God will always hear you."

"Do you think I could pray, Merlin? I've never done it before. We never went to church or anything. I never prayed before. Would God still listen to me?" Matthew asked.

"Gee, Matthew, I don't really know, but you can try. Just make sure you pray with all your heart and see what happens." Merlin answered. "Well, listen, I've got to get going. We'll see you tomorrow morning. Just come to the mouse door by the window on the south side of the big garage over there. Bye!"

Merlin ran home and went right to the kitchen. Millie and Morton both were there. He told them that Matthew had been thrilled to get the clothes and he and his family would be coming over for Christmas breakfast tomorrow. "They don't have any money at all, so they couldn't buy gifts for each other," he said. "Do you think if I prayed to God maybe God would ask Santa to bring them something too?"

"I don't know, dear," said Millie. Your prayers were answered last year. Try it. Just remember that God always knows best and sometimes what He, in His wisdom, decides isn't the same as what we think should happen."

That night, as Merlin lay in bed before going to sleep he thought, "I feel so happy when I think about God. I know that means He loves me.I know I can pray to Him, and if it is a cry of the heart, He will listen." So Merlin folded his paws together and prayed:

"Dear God, Matthew really needs help. Please, will you ask Santa Claus to bring presents for him and his mom and dad, and if it's not too much trouble some for me and my mom and dad too?"

Meanwhile, Matthew also was thinking about God. Earlier that evening, he had tried the clothes

Merlin had given him. They had fit perfectly, and Matthew felt all toasty warm and cozy now. His parents had also found that the clothes they had been given fit them, so they, too, were feeling much warmer. Matthew was trying to go to sleep, but his spirits fell when he remembered that he had nothing to give his parents on Christmas day. Then he recalled what Merlin had told him. Matthew didn't think praying would do any good at all, but Merlin had been so happy and positive about it that he thought it wouldn't hurt to give it a try.

As he lay on his little scrap of blanket, he folded his paws together and prayed:

"Dear God, Please, will you ask Santa Claus to bring presents for my mom and dad? They are so nice to me and I love them so much and if you don't help me, they won't have anything."

That night Matthew dreamed that God came to him. God speaks the language of every soul in creation, so God looked like a wise, old mouse with beautiful white fur and warm, loving eyes. God spoke to him in the kindest voice and said:

He loves us all,
whether big or small,
and listens well to
each heart's true call.
Just give it a try,

He's not far apart;
He's always as close
as the cry of your heart!
Never give up
and never despair,
where all is lost, God is there.
Call Him in need;
if your cry is true,
He will always be there for you.

The next morning Matthew and his family went to Merlin's house bright and early. Millie and Morton welcomed them in and served them warm, spiced cider in miniature porcelain cups they had salvaged from a discarded doll-sized tea set. They sat together in the bright, cheerful living room which was decorated with festive sprigs of holly and tiny pine cones. There was a large piece of evergreen set up as a Christmas tree. It was decorated with old earrings, strings of berries and bits of yarn and ribbon as well as other glittering things Millie had found.

Under the tree many beautifully wrapped little packages were placed. Merlin went over to the gifts and started reading the name tags on them. "There are two for Matthew," he said excitedly, "and two for me! Wow, that's great!" He gave two of the gifts to Matthew and then gleefully set about unwrapping his own.

Millie walked over to the gifts and found two with

Morton's name on them and gave them to him. Then, she said, "Look, here are two with the names 'Michael and Margaret' on them. Are those your names?" she asked, looking at Matthew's parents.

"Yes, they are," said Matthew's mom. And she and Matthew's dad happily took the gifts Millie handed them and started unwrapping them.

"And here are two for me," Millie said, smiling.

Soon the little room was full of joy as everyone unwrapped their gifts. Michael and Margaret got wonderful, warm scarves and mittens. Morton and Millie received little boxes of special chocolates and cheeses. Merlin found two little toy cars to go with the truck he had received last year and Matthew got a little sled with his name painted on it in bright red letters and a warm, hand-knitted cap to wear when he went sledding.

They all hugged each other and Merlin gave each of his parents a big kiss.

"I guess God heard me," Merlin said delightedly.

"And he heard me too!" said Matthew, beaming.

Millie brought out a wonderful breakfast of some pieces of different flavors of granola bars she had found at the mouse store. Merlin gathered his new cars and placed them carefully beside him. Matthew was so happy with his new cap that he had to put it on even though it was very warm inside, and he put his sled next to the little stool he was sitting on.

Morton told Michael that he was sure another cozy apartment could be found in the wall next to the big house just like the one they were living in. Michael was very excited about this, and they decided to go look for one right after breakfast.

Millie and Margaret shared happy, loving smiles as they looked at their families gathered around.

Margaret said, "We would like to give thanks to the Lord for His bounty and His Love which we have seen today and are so grateful to receive."

"Amen," said Millie and the others, as the spirit of Christmas filled the room around them with peace and joy.

Imani

oday was Kuumba, December 31st, the sixth day of Kwanzaa. Tonight was the Karamu Festival, the New Year's Eve of the Kwanzaa Celebration and tomorrow was Imani, January 1st, the last day of the celebration, the day for which Imani was named.

Imani, her mom, dad, grandma and older sister, Zenna, lived in a brownstone apartment building in Brooklyn, New York. Her older brother, Billy, was normally away at Princeton studying computer sciences but he was home now for the holidays.

Imani loved Kwanzaa. She loved having her family together. She loved the beautiful symbols and the delicious food. She also loved what each day of the seven-day holiday stood for: Umoja (Unity), Kujichagulia (Self-determination), Ujima (Collective work and responsibility), Ujamaa (Cooperative economics), Nia (Purpose), Kuumba (Creativity), and Imani (Faith).

On this day of Kuumba the family would gather to celebrate creativity first in its spiritual aspect and then in its physical, the creativity that uses thoughts to create new and better ways of living resulting in harmony and beauty.

In just about three hours the Kuumba celebration would start and then they'd have their Karamu feast. Dad and Billy were setting out the seven symbolic objects of Kwanzaa now — the Mazao or fruits, nuts and vegetables, the Mkeka or place mat, the Muhindi, or ears of corn, the Kinara or candleholder with its seven candles or Mishumaa saba, the Kikombe cha umoja or communal cup of unity and the Zawadi or gifts that would be given tomorrow.

Imani was headed toward the kitchen to see if mom and grandma needed any help. As she passed the living room she heard the sound of old movies coming from the TV. Zenna was a film major at N.Y.U. and watched classic movies as often as she could.

Although Imani's family was vegetarian, her mom and grandma prepared new and traditional dishes that were so delicious, all of Imani's friends begged her for invitations for weeks before the Karamu feast. Tonight their family would have fried tempeh with dumplings, black-eyed peas and rice, succotash, stewed okra, corn pudding, avocado and mandarin orange salad, mixed greens, pineapple upside-down cake and sweet potato pie.

As Imani walked into the kitchen, the smells were so delicious she could hardly wait for the feast to start. She asked her mom and grandma if there was anything she could do but they said, "Not now, maybe later."

Imani pulled up a chair and sat by the kitchen table. "Mom," she said. "Khalil's still bullying me like I told you and Gram about last week."

"Did you try what I told you?" asked her grandma.

"Yes," she replied. "I tried sending loving thoughts and praying he would get better, but nothing happened."

"Did you really mean it?" asked her mom.

"I tried to mean it," replied Imani. "But how could I? He's always clumping around trying to scare everyone and succeeding, too, because he's bigger than everyone else in our grade. He even stole Lateesha's lunch money from her."

"Did you ever try to understand his point of view?" asked her mom.

"What point of view!" Imani snorted. "He's a creep and a bully and that's all there is to it."

"But doesn't he live with just his uncle? I heard he's alone most of the time," said her mom.

"Yeah. So what?" said Imani.

"So he's probably lonely," said her mom. "And I know if his uncle's gone a lot there's probably nobody else around to give him love or guidance on what's right."

"We hurt ourselves if we think evil towards anyone else," Grandma said while kneading a batch of dough for whole wheat rolls. "The vibrations of our thoughts come back to us, so if we're thinking angry, hurtful thoughts, we're getting hurt. If we think loving thoughts, forgiving thoughts, compassionate thoughts, then we get love back. Plus by sending love to the other person we're helping them as well as ourselves," Grandma said.

"Maybe if Khalil didn't feel so lonely he'd be nicer," Mom said.

"And if pigs had wings they could fly!" said Imani sarcastically.

"If we pray to the Creator for the good of someone else and we pray sincerely, it will definitely have some helping effect," said Gram.

"Today is Kuumba — a day of creativity to help solve our difficulties. Today we celebrate the creative force of God in our lives. Try praying for him. See what happens," said Mom.

"Oh, okay," said Imani grumpily. "I will."

"But you have to mean it," said Gram, "or it won't work."

"Imani," said Mom. "The grocery store was out of whipping cream and I need a quart for topping on the sweet potato pie. Can you go to the Italian Market for me?"

"Sure, Mom," said Imani and went to put on her coat and boots. She ran happily down the stairs and out the door. Snow was falling gently. It covered the sidewalk and all the window ledges of the handsome brownstones that lined the street.

As she scuffed through the crisp snow towards the corner market, she saw Khalil farther down the block. Oh, no! Had he seen her? Could she cross over or run back the other way?

"Hey, Imani!" Khalil yelled.

"Too late," she thought.

"What're you doing out alone?" Khalil sneered. "Where's your keeper?"

"If you mean Lateesha, she's home with her family like you should be," Imani replied. "It's the Karamu feast tonight, you know." Too late she remembered Khalil probably didn't have any family to be at home with.

"Oh, I might drop by the Community Center later," he said in a mean voice, "or I might hang out with Dejohn. His older brother's always got something interesting for us if we can afford it."

"Khalil, you know you should take care of your health. That stuff'll mess you up!" Imani said fiercely.

"Like you care," Khalil replied with a sneer.

"I do care. You're a part of our community and each person is important. That's part of what Kwanzaa's about."

"You should be ashamed of lying like that, Imani. You know you don't mean a word of it," said Khalil. "Now — you got any money on you? Give it here; all of it!"

Imani prayed as hard as she could to God to help her send love — not hate and fear. Then she prayed to God to open Khalil's heart to receive love from her and from the Creator too.

All of a sudden she thought "What if he is lonely? What if he's ashamed of not having a family to be with tonight?"

"Khalil," she said. "I don't think you mean half the rotten stuff you say. I think you're really nice and afraid to show it. Would you come to my house for our Karamu feast? I'd really like for you to join us. Plus, tomorrow is Imani, the day I was named for, so that makes tonight even more special for me. Please will you come?"

Khalil looked stunned, then suspicious. "You mean it?"

"Yes. I really, really want you to come to our feast tonight," said Imani.

"Well, I don't know. Maybe...well, hey, I'm not doing anything all that important. Sure. I can drop by," said Khalil, trying not to show how pleased he was. "What time?"

"In about an hour," said Imani.

"Imani," said Khalil. "What does your name mean? All these years I've heard it and I always wondered."

"Faith," she said. "Faith in the power of our Creator's love." 🖌

Earth, Air, Fire & Water

Learning Love Stories

Pride and Humility

Once there were two sisters who lived with their family in a big house in a nice neighborhood in Delhi, India. One sister was named Pride and the other Humility.

One morning Pride told Humility that she had dreamed the night before of God, and God had told her He would visit her the next day. Humility told Pride that she also had dreamed of God and He had told her that He would visit her.

Pride said, "I'm the eldest. He will come to me first. I must get ready. I will wear my finest clothes and all my jewelry. I must look my best for God Himself."

Humility said, "I will wash the floor and the windows. Everything should be clean for Him. Then I will get fresh milk in case He would like some tea."

So Pride got dressed in her most beautiful clothing while Humility cleaned the house and went to the market to buy fresh milk to make chai tea, as well as sweets to serve along with the tea.

The morning passed, but God did not appear. Pride became more and more impatient and angry. "He told me He would visit me," she said. "It's not fair of Him to keep me waiting like this."

Humility waited patiently, sitting in meditation for much of the morning. "Time itself is a gift of God and I should use it to please Him," she said.

Soon it was lunch time. Pride walked angrily back and forth in the courtyard. Humility prepared chapatis and some delicious masala potatoes. "Since it is lunch time God may be hungry and I want to have something ready for Him," she said.

But He did not appear. "Please, dear sister, have something to eat with me," Humility said to Pride. The two sisters ate together after which Humility cleaned up. Pride sat looking angrily out the window in the living room, getting up once in awhile to open the door, look up and down the street and slam the door shut with a bang when nothing was there.

About 4 p.m. there was a knock at the door. Pride rushed to it, pushing Humility out of the way, and opened it wide. There was nobody there but a beggar.

"Please, kind young miss, I am so hungry. Do you have any food to spare?"

"For a dirty old beggar like you?" Pride said, "Absolutely not! I'm expecting God Himself, and you make my clean house look filthy. Go away and don't ever come back!" She slammed the door and sat again in the living room, waiting.

Humility went outside and down the street after the beggar. "This has been a very stressful day for my sister," she said to him. "Please forgive her and do come have a bite of food with us." She brought the beggar to their house and invited him into the kitchen where she gave him chapatis, masala potatoes, tea and sweets.

"Thank you, kind miss," the old beggar said happily and left.

At 5 p.m. there was a scratching at the door. Again Pride rushed to it and threw it open.

"It's a cat," she screamed. "A dirty, sneaky, ugly, mean old cat. Everyone knows that cats are cunning and they'll bite you if they get the slightest chance — what on earth is a dirty old cat doing here?"

"The cat looks hungry," said Humility. We still have food left over and it's almost time for dinner so I must prepare something fresh. Maybe the cat would like some of the milk or chapatis or potatoes."

"You're crazy, Humility," said Pride. "You do what you want but I will go to make sure my clothes and hair still look beautiful. The day isn't over yet. God said He would visit me today — I must be ready."

Humility poured some milk into a bowl, and tore a chapati into small pieces which she put on a plate with some of the leftover potatoes. She put the food out on the doorstep in front of the cat. The cat ate it eagerly and then drank the milk.

"You must have been very hungry," said Humility. "You look very thin. Please come and visit me whenever you want to. I will always give you something to eat because I know all animals are my younger brothers and sisters in the family of God." She petted the cat gently on the head and shut the door.

That evening their parents came home and the family had dinner together, visited awhile and went to bed.

As she got into bed Pride said, "I've never been so humiliated. I got my best clothes dirty and waited all day for nothing. I can't believe it, but God lied to me."

Humility said, "I had a wonderful day. Meditation made me feel calm and peaceful, plus I truly enjoyed making that poor, older gentleman happy by giving him something to eat. And the little cat was very hungry. It made me feel really good to see how much she appreciated the food I gave her. I hope she comes back again."

That night the two sisters went to sleep and dreamed the same dream. In the dream they both saw God.

"Why didn't you visit me?" asked Pride.

"I did visit you," said God. "I came in the form of an old beggar and again in the form of a cat, but you sent me away. Humility was the one who recognized me and served me."

Pride had a very hard time understanding what God meant. After awhile she understood it in theory, but she couldn't really understand it with her heart. She lived a sad and discontented life until, when she was quite old, she finally started feeling that everybody she met was worthy of her time, her courtesy, her concern and her kindness. Then, when she started behaving that way, her life became much happier.

Humility, on the other hand, had been lucky enough to understand what God meant right away. She went on knowing He was in everyone and being kind to everybody, so she lived happily ever after.

Bob Too

Amar lived with his parents, Vikram and Madoo, in a small apartment in Vijay Nagar, a suburb of Delhi, India. What Amar wanted most in the world was a bicycle — a shiny, new, red bicycle with gears. He knew his family was not wealthy and he would have to earn the money for it himself, so he asked his neighbor, Mr. Gulati the tailor, for an after-school job. Mr. Gulati was a kind man whose children were all grown up. He had nobody to run errands for him, and he was happy to give Amar the chance to earn a few rupees. So every afternoon, after school, Amar delivered parcels of new clothes to Mr. Gulati's customers. Finally, after working for almost a year and a half, he had enough money saved to buy just the bike he wanted.

One day Amar sat on the balcony of his family's second-floor apartment. He loved to watch the comings and goings on the street below — people going to or from work, children playing, and vendors passing by, crying out the names of the fruits and vegetables heaped high on their carts.

As he sat there, he saw a group of children. They

211

were screaming and shouting. As he looked closer he noticed they were throwing stones at something small. He ran down the stairs and up the street towards them. As he came closer he saw they were throwing stones at a frightened little puppy who was yelping in pain.

"Stop it!" he shouted. "Stop it!" But they wouldn't stop.

Amar ran to get help. He saw the mother of his best friend, Sumeet, coming along the dusty street. "Mrs. Taneja! Please help me!" he cried. "They're hurting a little dog." She hurried after him and quickly saw what the children were doing.

"Children! Stop that!" said Mrs. Taneja sternly. "If you hurt any living creature it will bring bad luck to you. Never, never hurt anyone!"

When they heard Mrs. Taneja and knew she recognized them, the children ran away.

"Poor puppy!" said Mrs. Taneja, as she watched Amar comfort it. "Amar," she continued, "I have to get home right away. I'm sorry I can't stay, but my mother isn't well. Can you take care of this little pup by yourself?"

"Sure I can," Amar said.

Amar carefully took the whimpering puppy into his arms. He carried him back home and washed the pup's wounds in clean water. Then he gave him some milk to drink – comforting him as best he could with soft pats and loving words.

When his parents came home they were quite concerned. "This animal is very badly hurt," said his mother.

"He needs to go to an animal clinic, and clinics are very expensive," said his father. "Where would we get the money to pay for it?"

"And even if we had the money," said his mother, "who would take care of him? I don't want a dog here. This apartment is too small for a pet."

Amar's eyes filled with tears. "I'll take care of him," Amar said fiercely. "I'll pay for his clinic care and medicine! I have the money I've been saving for my bike. I just can't stand the thought of his suffering and dying all alone."

"Are you sure you want to spend your money this way?" asked his father.

"Yes!" said Amar. "And I'll take care of him, honest! When he's all better we can see if I can keep him or not. Okay? Dad? Mom?"

"All right," said his father.

"All right for now," said his mother.

So Amar took the little dog to the animal clinic where he watched Dr. Jain take care of the pup. The veterinarian gently stitched up a nasty cut. Then Dr. Jain gave Amar a pot of salve to put on the wounds to help them heal better. "Take care of him now and he'll thank you for it later," said Dr. Jain with a smile.

As Amar tended to the little dog, they grew to love and trust one another. He named the puppy Bob Too after Bob, Son of Battle, a story book he'd read in the school library about a Scottish sheep dog. It was one of his favorite books because the dog in it was so noble and such a good friend to the family he belonged to. It always gave Amar a warm feeling when he read that book and he'd always thought how nice it would be to have a friend like that. Now he did have one and it gave him a very warm feeling whenever he thought about it.

Amar took care of Bob Too's wounds every morning before school, and again when he came home from his after-school job. He gently took the bandages off and washed the dog's wounds carefully. Then he applied the ointment that Dr. Jain had given him and rewrapped the wounds in clean bandages.

Soon Bob Too was healed and well. One day Amar's mother said it was time to look for a new home for him.

"But Mom!" Amar cried, "Bob Too is part of our family now. He's a good dog and my friend."

"I warned you, Amar. This house is too small for a dog. And that's the last I'll say about it."

Heartbroken, Amar ran to his room. He was crying. He gave Bob Too a big hug. Then through his tears, he prayed: "Oh, God, it is said that You hear the cry of an ant if the cry is from its heart. Please, hear me — please, please help us."

Amar woke up with a start late that night. There was a loud crash and the sound of furious barking coming from the living room. Everyone else was awake too. Vikram, Madoo and Amar ran from their rooms to see what had happened.

There in the living room they found Bob Too growling and shaking a piece of cloth in his sharp little teeth. They saw a man climbing over the balcony railing who ran off down the street. When they turned on the light they found that Bob Too had a scrap of the man's trousers, and that the windows by the balcony had been forced open.

"Amar," said his father, "Bob Too has just saved us from being robbed! As of right now, I hereby officially declare that Bob Too is a real member of this family!"

"Yes," said Madoo, "Bob Too stays." She petted his head and scratched behind his ears. "He doesn't really take up much room," she said, smiling.

Amar was very happy for awhile but sometimes as he delivered his parcels, trudging along the hot, dusty streets, he got to thinking about the bicycle that he would have had if he hadn't spent all his money on helping Bob Too. "It will take another whole year before I can earn the money again to buy a bike," he grumbled, kicking at the dust as he walked along.

As time went by, thoughts of the bicycle began to prey on his mind. He still loved Bob Too but he

thought maybe he had been foolish to sacrifice so much just to help an animal. "After all," he thought, "I could have found a healthy puppy and then I could have spent my money on a new bike like I'd planned to. But my teacher says: You never lose anything when you give. You always get something back. Bob Too needed help so much. If I hadn't helped him he would have suffered so badly and maybe died. I didn't know him at all then but now I love him so much. I guess I really did do the right thing and I'm just going to stop thinking about that stupid bicycle."

That evening when he got home, tired and dusty after doing his chores, he saw a new red collar with a tag on it that read "Bob Too" lying on the kitchen table, and standing in the corner there was a shiny red bicycle with gears! There was a note tied to it which read:

> *Dear Amar,*
>
> *Thanks to Bob Too for saving us,*
> *and thanks to you for saving*
> *Bob Too!*
> *We love you both!*
>
> *Mom & Dad*

Unity Begins
With You

Jimmy unlocked his bike from the bike stand on the edge of the playground and started to ride over to the Baskin-Robbins on the corner to get an ice-cream cone on his way home. He saw Stanislas, the kid who'd just come over from one of those countries whose names he could never remember. Stanislas was walking on the other side of the street way down, past the intersection.

"Hey, Stan's-a-loser, how's it feel to be a wetback-keep back?" he shouted. Stanislas didn't say anything, but he looked back at Jimmy and smiled timidly.

"You, loser, I'm talking to you!" Jimmy shouted. "Whatsa matter, loser, don't ya understand English?" Again, Stanislas didn't reply but, instead, smiled a strained and sort of hopeful smile.

Jimmy was big for his age and Stanislas was smaller and slightly built. Jimmy glared at him and said, "What makes you think you belong here, you little creep? I'll teach you where you belong!" Jimmy shook his fist angrily and started pedaling as fast as he could towards the smaller boy.

Stanislas was scared but stood his ground

waiting for Jimmy to come down the block to him. All of a sudden there was a loud crash, and a scream pierced the air. Stanislas saw, to his amazement, that Jimmy hadn't noticed the car making a left turn across the intersection. Instead of stopping at the curb, Jimmy had kept right on pedaling furiously. The car had hit the boy on the bike and kept right on going, driving away at top speed. The bike was a tangled mess of spokes and metal and Jimmy was lying on the street in a heap.

Stanislas ran down the street to where Jimmy was lying. He knelt down and gently touched him. "Are you all right?" Stanislas asked.

Jimmy opened his eyes and shook his head as if dazed. He tried to stand up but, instead, exclaimed in pain and fell back down. "What's wrong?" Stanislas asked.

"I think I broke my foot or sprained my ankle or something. It hurts so bad I can't stand up on it. And my bike's a real mess. I don't know how I'll get home," Jimmy said.

Stanislas helped Jimmy over to the sidewalk. "I'll run back to school and get the gym teacher. Mr. Jordan will know what to do," he said, starting back towards the school.

Within ten minutes Mr. Jordan drove up. He and Stanislas got out of the car. Mr. Jordan looked at Jimmy's ankle and foot and decided it was a sprain.

"I'll put your bike in the trunk and drive you home, Jimmy. You keep ice on it tonight and if it isn't better by tomorrow your mom can take you to the clinic. Come on, let's go," and he helped Jimmy up and towards the car.

Jimmy felt really embarrassed. He knew he would have been in big trouble without the other boy's help. "Hey, guy," said Jimmy. "Thanks! If you hadn't helped me, who knows how long I'd have been lying there. You want to come over and have some microwave popcorn with me while I put ice on this ankle?"

"That would be really nice," Stanislas replied, smiling.

Later, Jimmy sat at the kitchen table with his foot propped up on a chair and an ice pack around his ankle. "How come you helped me even when I was so mean to you?" he asked the other boy as he reached for a handful of popcorn.

Stanislas shrugged. "I knew you didn't really mean what you were saying," he said. "I knew it was just because I'm new here and don't talk like you do or dress the same. I didn't like what you said, but I couldn't leave you in bad trouble."

"Well, it was okay of you," Jimmy said. "Really okay. But, if I can ask, how come you do dress so funny and talk so strange?"

"There was a lot of fighting in my country. It was

like a war but it wasn't called a war. There were bombs all the time. One of them destroyed our house. My mom and dad and I escaped with only what we were wearing when the alert sounded.

"We spent months in a camp with almost no food, no water and one blanket for all of us. Then we heard that some of us could get out through help from a church here in your country, so we did. We were lucky — we got out — but here we're really poor. We have some clothes the church gave us that people donated. They don't fit so well, but it's a lot better than nothing. We're really grateful. My mom and dad are both working, but they need training to get better jobs in this country. Now they don't earn much. We almost can't pay rent and buy food, so we really can't afford better clothes. And, even though I learned English in my country in school, still I have the accent...."

"That was really tough, Stan," said Jimmy. "By the way, can I call you Stan?"

Stanislas nodded, smiling.

"I should've thought about what it was like for you before I said all that mean stuff," said Jimmy. "If I went through all you did I don't know if I could be as brave. Or as nice. Thanks for helping me even after I was so stupid."

"We all make mistakes," said Stanislas. "If I forgive you maybe I can have a friend some day instead of an enemy. I've seen in my country what enemies and war and suffering can do. Hey — do you know how to play football?"

"I sure do!" said Jimmy smiling. "You want to toss a football around?"

"I'd like that a lot," Stanislas said.

"Of course, you'll have to wait a while," said Jimmy and the two of them laughed, together.

The Magic Circle

oyce was reading a library book in the fading afternoon light. Her brother, Jamie, was doing something at the family's computer. It sounded to Joyce like a Dungeons and Dragons game.

Their mom came in and asked if they had clean clothes to wear to the school play that night.

"Yes," answered Joyce.

"I dunno," mumbled Jamie.

"Could you go and look now, please," said his mom. "I want to get any washing finished now because we'll be gone all evening and tomorrow is very busy."

"Aw, Mom," grumbled Jamie.

"Now!" said his mom firmly.

"Mom," said Joyce.

"Yes?" replied her mom.

"In values class last week, Mrs. Jones gave our weekly lesson and homework on helping others and there were some things I wondered about...."

"What, dear?" asked her mom.

"Well," said Joyce, "Mrs. Jones told us that

helping others selflessly was anything you did that helped anyone — human or animal — for which you didn't receive any selfish benefit. But then she said that selflessly helping others gave you, as a reward for doing it, the greatest benefit of all — happiness. Then she said that lots of things counted as helping others like helping clean up after meals, or helping carry something if someone had too much to carry by themselves. Taking time to talk to somebody, maybe someone new in the neighborhood or school, or somebody elderly who might be lonely; or finding a stray animal a home — there was a long list."

"So what's your question, sweetie?" asked her mom.

"Well," said Joyce. "I don't like to clean up after meals; I want to talk with Katie and Sue on the phone or read. And I don't like to talk to elderly people — it's boring. And I don't want to help anybody carry things, or help weed the garden, or say something extra nice to cheer up someone who's sad, or be friendly to new people, or, actually, any of the stuff she mentioned. So I haven't done even one thing (that was our homework assignment) and I just wondered what you thought about it all."

"Yeah, Mom," said Jamie who'd returned with a small pile of dirty clothes.

"Okay, kids. This is kind of a hard one, but here goes. Do you think I like doing your dirty laundry?

Jamie? Joyce?"

"I never thought about it," said Jamie.

"Me neither," said Joyce.

"So think about it now, and tell me," said their mom, smiling.

"You must like it cause you've been doing it for years and you never make a fuss or sound unhappy," said Jamie.

"I love you both," said their mom, "and even though I work downtown and do all the home stuff myself, too, I want you to have clean clothes. So even though I'm really tired sometimes, I do your laundry as a service to you because I love you. Sometimes, in fact a lot of the time, I don't really want to do it. Sometimes I'd rather sit down and read a book myself. But knowing that I'm doing something to help you both makes me feel happy in a different way."

"What kind of way?" asked Joyce.

"It's like a magic circle," said their mom. "It's invisible to the eyes of mortal men and women, but inside the circle the faery folk play their magic flutes and a beautiful music sings to your soul and gives you such delight."

"Are you serious? It sounds like you've been playing Dungeons and Dragons!" said Jamie with a big smile.

"Well, of course, what I'm telling you is an illustration of how it works, not actual reality, but a magic circle is the closest way I can come to telling you the truth," said their mom. "When you do something to help somebody, it's like you step inside the magic circle within you. It doesn't have to be a big, hard thing — any act of kindness — no matter how small, qualifies.

"Any caring word or deed makes the world a better place. And, as you get into it, it becomes more and more of a habit and the magic grows and grows. Sometimes what you are doing to help somebody may seem a bit hard or boring, but the magic gives you a wonderful reward, a special joy, a happiness, a delight. After a while, that wonderful, sweet happiness is something you really look forward to, so helping others becomes something you want to do."

"But when I helped Mr. Thane with the garden weeds I hated it," said Joyce.

"And when I helped Mrs. Ridley with all those groceries, I hated it too," said Jamie.

"Maybe you were so certain you would hate it, that you closed your hearts to the magic so you couldn't feel it," said their mom. "And sometimes you feel the magic later, not right away, and different people feel it differently. Or maybe you tried to do too much all at one time. 'Rome wasn't built in a day.'"

"What do you mean?" asked Joyce.

"Each of us is so much the same," said her mom, "but each of us is also different. If you're trying to learn how to do something new you have to learn it little by little and start learning it in the ways that are easiest for you. Helping others is always good and if the reason for it is an emergency or a necessity of some kind, then it's really good to build up the muscles of your ability to help — your response-ability, but emergencies don't happen all the time. And there are so many ways to help others that might involve something you'd enjoy, if you gave it half a chance and didn't close your heart before you even tried."

"Like what?" asked Joyce.

"Okay. You said your homework was to do one nice thing for someone else, just one act of service, and you said you hadn't done it yet. Why don't you do the laundry for me, and let me sit down and read a book for a change?"

"Mom!" moaned Joyce, "I don't want to do the laundry. I'm almost done with this book and I really want to finish it."

"But that's where the magic circle starts, sweetie," said her mom. "You have to break the habit that keeps you always thinking only of yourself and think of someone else for a change. And when you start to think of others more and yourself a little less, the magic circle within you stretches bigger and bigger and you start feeling more and more happy."

"So if I do the laundry now, you could relax a little and that would make you happy. Then making you

happy would make me happy. Is that it?" asked Joyce.

"I could help and that would show you how much I appreciate all the stuff you always do for us," said Jamie, thoughtfully. "We really do appreciate you, Mom."

"The magic circle works best if you really want to help. If you do it because you feel you have to, it won't work at all the same, though sometimes you might catch a few notes of the music or smell the fragrance of the flowers that are always blooming there," said their mom.

"Okay. I'll try it. I love you, Mom, and I'd like to see you relax more and have a bit of quiet time for yourself," said Joyce, putting her book down and picking up the dirty clothes and heading for the washing machine.

"I'll help sort and fold," said Jamie, shutting down the computer and following after her.

Later that evening as Joyce, Jamie and their mom left to go to the school play, Joyce handed her mother a fresh, fragrant, gorgeous red rose.

"Where did you get this, Joyce?" asked her mom. "It's almost winter now."

"I found it blooming in the magic circle," said Joyce.

"It was really neat in there," said Jamie, laughing with delight at the look on his mom's face. 🪶

A Crying Time

It was almost dinner time when I got home and saw the light in the kitchen shining out through the windows. It turned the snow on the bushes into powdered sugar diamonds. When I walked in I saw mom at the kitchen table. She had a cup of tea and she was looking at a piece of paper. She'd been crying.

"What is it, Mom?" I asked. "What's wrong?"

"It's Sue," she said and broke down into tears again.

My father had died of kidney failure when I was thirteen. My sister, Sue, was just two days away from her ninth birthday. It was bad for all of us but worse for Mom because just out of nowhere she felt there was nobody to take care of her and she had to take care of both of us.

"Oh, Ted," she started, and then choked up again.

All of a sudden I was really worried.

What could it be? She'd been so strong, so loving; always there for both of us. It had been three years now. I didn't see her crying at all anymore, but I

233

remembered back then we all cried a lot for a long time. Some days I thought I'd never be happy again.

"Unhappy times come to us all," our Spiritual Teacher told us. "You have to have faith that God loves you. You have to focus on whatever good you can find, and remember — there is light at the end of the tunnel. No matter how bad it seems, it won't last forever. And, most of all — meditate! When you go deep in prayer into the silence within you, you come in contact with the inner Light and it fills you with peace, with strength and with joy. When you come back, that peace and joy stays with you."

We all sat together for meditation in the early mornings back then and it did help. Though it was still hard.

Mom went back to work. "If I can keep us in a place to live with food to eat and clothes to wear and see to it that you and Sue get your education, I'll know I've done what's right," she used to say.

Was Sue doing okay at school? Did she need something medical we couldn't afford? Why was Mom crying? I'm working after school each day and that helps, but it's still tight. "What is it, Mom?" I asked. "Why won't you tell me?"

"Oh, Ted," she started, and then got up from the table, crying again. "Wait," she said. "I'll be right back." and she left the room.

I remember how alone she told me she felt back then.

She used to talk to me a little after Sue was in bed. "Be patient about how you feel and don't try to go too fast. Just focus on one thing at a time," our Spiritual Teacher had told her, and she told me that helped.

I know I was pretty angry, as well as sad, when Dad died. "Everything that happens, happens for our highest good, though from our limited human level of understanding, sometimes we can't see that," our teacher told me. "We can go through sad times more easily if we focus on our faith in God and remember the love He has for us." When I kept that advice in my mind I found it helped almost like magic.

"Mom?" I called. "Are you coming back here?"

I remembered how some of the men at the Interfaith Center we belong to had invited me out to baseball games with their families. One of them learned I liked to write poetry and started corresponding with me regularly — sharing poems back and forth. That meant such a lot to me and I know it made Mom happier to see me happy.

But what could have her so upset now? Just the other day she told me she finally felt that the love God was giving her was so strong she didn't feel alone or unloved at all. "Meditation makes me feel like I live in an enchanted garden. Following the rules God wants us to live by puts a fence all around the garden protecting it from rabbits eating the lettuce and deer nibbling the young leaves. I feel so loved — maybe more loved — than when my Ben was still alive," she told me.

So what could it be? She doesn't start crying out of nowhere any more like she used to. She was so afraid she'd mess up our lives by being a single parent. She was afraid she couldn't give us the love, help and guidance she could have if Dad had still been with us. "Put in your best effort and leave the rest to God," our Spiritual Teacher told us. I know that advice helped me a lot and it helped her too.

"When I meditate I feel the love of God so strong," she told me. "It's like taking a vacation in heaven. And when I try to do my best and leave the rest to God it just takes all the anxiety and guilt away."

So what could have done this to her now? Where was she? What could be so bad she wouldn't talk about it after all we've gone through? Could it have something to do with the piece of paper lying there on the table by her cup? I picked up the paper and read:

English Assignment —Write About A Hero

My Hero
By Sue Hart
My mom is my hero because every day she goes to work even when she doesn't want to. She has bad things to deal with but she does it. She drives a long way to work and then back.

Then, when she gets home she gets dinner for my brother and me even when she's really tired.

My mom is my hero because she meditates and helps me to meditate, too. She has taught me to think everything happens for our highest good and we should have faith in God.

I miss Dad but I know he loves me and Ted and Mom. When I meditate I feel his love and God's love, too.

My mom is my hero.

Just then Mom came back.

"Oh, Ted, did you read that?" she said.

"Yeah, Mom, but why were you crying?" I asked.

"They were tears of joy. It made me so happy," she said.

"Oh, Mom," I laughed.

"Oh, Ted," she said and smiled.

"Good night — I love you," we said almost exactly at the same time.

She turned off the kitchen light. By then the moon had come up and it shone in through the window. I could hear the geese who'd stayed through the winter down on the pond and I knew tomorrow would be a really good day.

Selfish Steam

Mom," shouted Jane. "Jane, how many times have I asked you not to shout?" replied her mom from the next room.

"But, Mom, I'm in real trouble," whined Jane. "Jane, how many times have I helped you? Don't I always help you? Your problems matter to me. What is it?" asked her mom.

"We're studying self-esteem in school and we're supposed to write at least one page illustrating our understanding of it, but I don't understand it," said Jane.

"What don't you understand?" her mom asked.

"I don't understand it enough to even understand what I don't understand," said Jane.

"What do you think 'self-esteem' is?' asked her mom.

"Miss Druid told us it was respecting ourselves and being aware of what was good about ourselves. But what if you don't feel good about yourself?" Jane asked slowly.

"Don't you feel good about yourself?" asked her mom.

"Well... No, I don't. I'm not all that smart. I don't have any special talents like singing or dancing. I'm not rich. I don't dress better than anyone else. I have a few friends, but I'm not super popular like the cheerleaders are. So what is there to feel good about?"

"Jane, sweetie," said her mom, coming over and putting an arm around her, "I never realized you felt so unhappy with yourself. Honey, do you remember when you were little and I told you the story of the two hands?" her mom asked.

"I don't, actually," said Jane.

"Once there were two hands..." her mom started.

"Do I have to listen to a kid's story?" asked Jane, heaving a big sigh.

"Yes, in this case you do. Get yourself some juice or something and get me some, too, please — this is something we have to spend as much time with as it takes."

"Once there were two hands," her mom continued. "The two hands got along fine until one day the thumb on the right hand said it was bigger than the thumb on the left hand and made fun of the left thumb for being such a weak little thing. Then the ring finger on the right hand said the ring finger on the left hand was only meant to wear a wedding ring and it could wear jewelry any time, so it was better. The little finger of the left hand had been injured and had lost its fingernail, so the little finger of the right hand said it was more beautiful and better because the other finger ruined it for everyone when the nails wanted to wear fingernail polish. And on and on it went. Somehow it just grew out of proportion. Finally, the right hand said it was in every way the better hand, so it would no longer associate with something as ugly and unrefined as the left hand.

" 'I don't need you,' the right hand said scornfully.

"Well, the left hand believed what the right hand said. Of course it should have been obvious that the right hand was being much too snobbish and critical. But the left hand felt so wretched that it tried to hide in a pocket all the time, while the right hand wore a lot of rings and showed off about how smart and beautiful it was.

"One day, the two hands went to typing class. The right hand sat on top of the keyboard just as proud as a peacock, and the left hand hid below the typing table in a pocket. But, try as it might, the right hand couldn't type well without the left hand. Then, as they left school that day, the right hand found it couldn't carry all the books and still open the door either.

"That night the right hand apologized to the left hand. 'I'm sorry,' it said. 'I didn't realize — I guess I do need you, after all. Well, you do all the hard and dirty work, and I'll do all the smart and fun work. You'll have the reward of helping someone as beautiful and wonderful as me. What do you say?'

"Of course, the right hand didn't feel sorry at all. It was just trying to get the left hand to do what it wanted. The right hand was still too full of pride — I call it selfish steam — to realize how ridiculous it sounded. But the left hand was too full of hurt feelings to see how bossy and silly the right hand was, so the left hand said, 'I'm too ugly and slow. I won't help anyone.' Neither one of them understood that God has created the world to be full of diversity on purpose and we all need each other. We have to help each other before we can get along in harmony and live happy lives the way God has intended us to.

"The right hand said, 'But I need you. I command you to do it.'

"The left hand said, 'I just want to be left alone.'"

Jane interrupted, laughing, "Mom I love you, but your stories get pretty long-winded sometimes. Though I do see what you mean, I think."

Jane's mom laughed, too, and then continued, "The point is both hands were needed. They were different, but one was not better. The left hand should not have accepted the right hand's criticism which was based on egotism and pride. The right hand should have realized that different is not deficient.

"Finally, the right hand realized how important the left hand's help was, and it saw how nasty and bossy it was acting. Then it apologized sincerely and the left hand listened because the right hand was finally talking really nicely. They started cooperating and were able to get a lot done together. They saw how wonderful it was to work together with mutual respect and harmony, and they lived that way happily ever after."

"Great ending, Mom!" laughed Jane. "And I really get what you mean, too. I'm okay the way I am. I shouldn't see my differences as deficiencies. Maybe other people are more popular or do something that looks more important, but I have other strengths and I can use them to contribute something positive."

"Jane that's exactly it!" said her mom, happily. "And here's something else important, too. Do you exist when you're alone?"

"What a question!" exclaimed Jane. "Of course I do."

"And who are you when you're alone?" asked her mom.

"Hmmm. That's something I've never thought about." said Jane.

"Well, it's not easy to understand right away, but think about it a bit, and it'll make sense. To really find out, you have to see who you are when you're in prayer, when you're in meditation, because that's when you're most aware of God's love and your higher self shines out.

"When you experience His love, you know you're never really alone. Then you have the strength to hold onto the knowledge of your higher self for longer and longer. Even if other people act like they don't respect you or value you, you feel secure in your own self-respect because it's based on something stable — the love of God."

"Mom, that sounds wonderful, but it's so different from how I feel now," said Jane.

"I know, sweetie," said her mom. "If I meditate every morning, the Light gives me so many good things. I experience God's Love and, because I feel happy, it's easier to get along with others in harmony. Sometimes, if someone is really hard to get along with, or the day is really difficult, I lose sight of it, but I know when I meditate it'll come back again."

There was a comfortable silence as Jane and her mom sat together, sipping their juice. Then Jane said, "Do you remember how I saved that little bird who hit the window and was knocked unconscious?"

"I do," said her mom.

"It felt so great to help a little, living creature. And when I found a home for that stray kitten, or when I gave some of my clothes to that girl who didn't have many. I felt beautiful then. I didn't think at all then about what I look like, or what other people might be saying about me. I was concentrating so hard on how best to help — I felt so wonderful, so happy."

"That's it, Jane," said her mom. "When you are true to your higher self, you do feel wonderful."

Jane jumped up out of her chair and threw her arms around her mom. "You're probably the greatest mom on earth, maybe in the galaxy!" she said. "I'm going to write about all this for my homework. Oh, Mom, I love you!" she said and ran off to write her paper.

Esperanza Means Hope

Juan and Rosa were weeding the small patch of garden where their mother had planted tulips and daffodils last fall when they had first moved to this country. They had found a small, older house in a still-very-nice neighborhood right away. "Now we have a home!" Mamá had said gaily.

"Mamá wants every weed out!" said Rosa.

"I know, I know," said Juan."

"Juan," said Rosa, "You know our Grandmamá is dying, don't you?"

"Of course I know, stupid, do you think I've been hiding every time Mamá talks to Papá about it?" said Juan sarcastically.

"But it's been three months now and Mamá still doesn't have the money to fly to Perú to say good-bye."

"I know," said Juan.

"Even with her extra job and Papá driving two shifts, still it's not enough," said Rosa.

"But why are you telling me, Rosa? I can't do anything," said Juan, shrugging his shoulders like Papá did when he was upset but wished to look strong.

"I'm telling you because we must be extra nice

to Mamá," said Rosa. "When Aunt María called three months ago telling her Grandmamá had cancer and the doctors said all the children should come to say good-bye, Mamá was sure she would have the money in time to go. But she doesn't. This will be a very sad time for her. Let's do everything we can to cheer her up. And stop calling me stupid, stupid!"

"I'm home, Rosalita! Qué pasa, Juan?" called their father, Pedro, walking strong and tall down the sidewalk toward them. "Juan, Rosalita, I have wonderful news! The cab company gave me a bonus for being the driver with the best safety record for this quarter! I think it will be enough for Mamá's ticket," said Pedro, excitedly.

"Kids, I'm home!" said their mother. She walked up the sidewalk, put her arm around Pedro and looked at the small patch of garden. "What a wonderful job you've done," she said. "All the weeds are gone and only the beautiful tulips and daffodils are left! They are like bright flames of hope, each one of them!"

"Like you are, Esperanza," said Pedro tenderly. "And speaking of hope, you'll never guess what has happened."

"What, corazón?" asked Esperanza.

"The cab company has given me a $300.00 bonus for being their safest driver this quarter," said Pedro. "I hope if we combine it with what you've already saved, it will be enough for your ticket to Perú."

"Oh, Pedro, I know the figures by heart. It is enough. I'll call the airlines immediately! I think, with the grace of God, I'll get there in time." And Esperanza flew up the stairs, through the door and to the telephone!

All the family gathered around as she called. They saw that she looked hopeful but then very sad. As she hung up the phone she said, "Because it is high season, all the flights to South America are booked for one month solid. The best I can do is get a standby ticket for tonight. It's not certain, not at all, but the ticket agent was hopeful."

"Surely the gracious God will know that it is for love and virtue that you wish to go and He will extend His hand and you will get on!" said Pedro, smiling.

That night Esperanza, taking only a carry-on with the necessities, went to the airport with Pedro, Juan and Rosa. As they waited at the gate, all of the ticketed passengers were boarded and then all of the standbys except for Esperanza.

Desperately she went to the desk and explained to the airline personnel that she absolutely had to get on this flight, as it was the only possibility she had of getting back home to see her mother before her mother passed away.

The personnel were sympathetic but firm. Every single seat was filled. The flight attendants had even given their own seats away and would be sitting on the folding jump seats for the entire flight. They were very sorry but absolutely nothing could be done.

Esperanza pleaded with them, tears flowing down her cheeks, but there was, finally, no hope. After the plane had taken off, Esperanza, Pedro, Juan and Rosa went dejectedly home.

There, gathered around the kitchen table, they all tried to comfort a heartbroken and sobbing Esperanza. "But how could God do this to me?" she sobbed. "I've tried so hard to be good. I've tried so hard to live as He tells me to. Why didn't He care enough to help me? Why has He done this?"

"No, no, Esperanza," said Pedro, "Don't you remember? It is God who knows what is best for us, not us. It is God who sees everything and gives what is for our highest good. You can't have forgotten that. Try to understand it, querida mía. It is God who gave us the way to come here, and this nice house, and the jobs we have, and two strong, loving children. It is God who has given us so many blessings. Just because He didn't give us this one thing we wanted that is no reason to stop trusting Him. Yes, it is very hard for us and very sad, but all life and all things belong to Him."

Esperanza listened patiently as Pedro spoke, but she was too filled with grief to really hear what he was saying. When he had finished speaking she burst out crying and said, "God is my protection, my hope, my life. I have always trusted that He knows best, but I was wrong. Now I see I was wrong; He doesn't care about me. He couldn't love me and deny me the only way to see mi madre before she dies."

"No, no, queridísima, you are hurt and frightened so you strike out at the One who loves you like a little child, but try to understand. Try to remember all the other times there were hard things to go through and they all turned out alright, often even better than before," said Pedro tenderly.

"Mamá," said Rosa softly. "You are always telling me when things are bad for me, or sad, or scary, I should stop and meditate...I should pray. Have you forgotten?"

"Yes, Mamá," said Juan. "You and Papá always tell us the Light will clear away the darkness of fear and pain."

"You're right, you're right. All of you are right. It's just that it hurts so horribly, terribly much."

"Come on, querida. Out of the mouths of babes..." said Pedro.

They sat right there at the kitchen table, their heads bowed in prayer, in meditation.

After some time Esperanza opened her eyes. "You were right, Pedro," said Esperanza. "I did feel peace. I feel so different now. I felt God's love. How could I have forgotten? He knows better with all His vast wisdom than I do. He holds all life and death in His Love. We aren't at His level; we can't understand what happens the way He does. Every soul on earth has a time to live and a time to die. In the Light I remembered death is not a final parting. I leave it to Him for what He considers best. I leave it to Him completely. Whatever He wills."

Pedro put his arms around her and kissed her.

Rosa said, "I'll make us all some tea."

"I'll cut a big bouquet of daffodils and tulips," said Juan.

"Daffodils are for hope and tulips are for love," said Esperanza.

The next morning, as they were eating breakfast, the phone rang.

"It's Aunt María," said Rosa.

Esperanza talked with her sister and then, hanging up the phone, turned to her family and said, "You won't believe it, mi madre has taken a turn for the better. The doctors are saying she was misdiagnosed. It wasn't cancer! She will live."

"A miracle!" said Rosa.

"I was so sad when I couldn't fly to see mi madre," said Esperanza, half smiling, half weeping with joy. "I couldn't understand how God could do such a thing to me, but now we learn she will not die, after all; she will recover and because I could not go, we have the money from my ticket to fly her here. After she is all better, she can come and see our house and visit her grandchildren. How happy she will be!"

"The gracious Lord does hear our prayers, and He does know best," said Pedro. "Thank God!"

"Yes, Pedro," said Esperanza, "Thank God always!"_

The Nothing Gift

Pete and his sister, Liz, and his mom and dad lived in an old house on a small farm in the country near Bowling Green, Virginia. Like many small farmers, Pete's dad couldn't earn a living farming anymore, but wanted his son and daughter to grow up with plenty of fields, trees and clean air around them. There weren't a lot of jobs available because there was no industry, but his dad worked as a deliveryman and his mom worked part-time in the drugstore in town so there was always enough, just not a lot of extra.

Pete and his family were mostly pretty happy, though Pete wished his family's car wasn't so old and beaten-up, or that he could have a new bicycle instead of the old one he had. Sometimes, Pete wished that he had a newer jacket or nicer clothes like most of the other kids.

One day he went to his mom and asked, "Why do they have so much and we have so little? Why is all their stuff new and all ours old?"

"I know it must be hard for you, Pete," his mom replied. "But it's not what you have that counts — it's what you are, what you think, what you feel, and what you do. Can you buy a smile, Pete? Can you buy laughter or a happy heart?"

"I know I do feel pretty happy most of the time, but I still wish we had more money," Pete said.

"But we have enough, Pete," his mom said. "We just don't have a lot of extra. That's what God thinks is best for us right now. There's nothing wrong in having new things if you can afford them. But there's nothing wrong in not having them either. We've got nothing to be ashamed of. We earn our living honestly and we share what we can to help others who have even less than we do. And when we're grateful for what we do have and try to help others who have less, God gives us a lot of love and a lot of joy.

"Our family has always loved each other, and we've always been able to show our affection for each other, so you don't know what it's like not to have that, but that's what God has given us. I'll tell you this, Pete — God gives everything that is truly best for everyone even though sometimes we can't see exactly why. And nobody gets lasting happiness from things. Sometimes rich people are the most unhappy. If people have a lot of costly things but they aren't grateful for them or caring and sharing with others, they aren't happy, not in their heart of hearts, they aren't — I guarantee it."

Pete trusted his mom enough to believe her. But

her birthday was coming up and he didn't have enough money to buy her a present. Usually he mowed lawns or raked leaves or did other errands to earn spending money, but nobody had hired him for quite awhile and he didn't have any money at all.

He knew the grocery store in town would pay people for any game or fish they caught because the store had a specialty business selling fresh meat and fish to the rich people who lived on the hill. Pete and his family were vegetarians, but he thought maybe it would be okay to try to catch some of the trout he knew were in the lake close to his house — not to eat, he wouldn't do that — but to sell.

So one day, after school, he borrowed a fishing pole from a friend and went to the lake to see if he could catch some trout. He saw several fish swimming there and set his line and waited. After awhile he felt a fish bite and pulled it out of the water. But as he looked into the lake he saw four smaller fish swimming around sort of frantically as if they were really upset. "Good grief," he thought, "could this fish I've caught be the mother of those little ones?"

He thought awhile and then decided, "I need money for a gift for my mother, but how can I enjoy any money I earn by hurting the mother of other living creatures?" So he put the big fish back and watched as that fish and the smaller ones leaped happily together and then swam away.

The next night was his mother's birthday party. He still hadn't been able to earn any money to buy her anything, so he wrote down what had happened with the fish and called the story "The Nothing Gift." Then he put the story in an old shoe box and wrapped the box with paper from the saved wrapping paper and ribbon bag and put it on the dinner table next to the other gifts.

It was great to have the family together, and the lentil loaf, mashed potatoes, mushroom gravy and vegetables seemed especially delicious. Pete, Liz and their dad had baked an eggless cake and decorated it with silver sparkles and candles. After singing happy birthday and eating the wonderful cake, his mom opened her three presents.

She'd gotten a beautiful locket from dad and she loved it. She got a hand-knitted vest from Liz, which she put on right away. Then she opened Pete's gift. At first she seemed a little surprised, but then, as she read the story, her face looked so happy Pete's heart leaped for joy.

"I'd rather have this 'nothing gift' than anything else I can think of, Pete," she said. "It shows you care about other living creatures and that shows you care about your dad and me and what we've tried to teach you. I'd rather have a loving, caring family than any other gift in the whole world. Thank you!"

"If you make others happy, you will be happy," his dad said, smiling. "Today you've made your mom and me so happy and yesterday you made a mother fish and four young ones happy also. I'm really proud of you."

Pete's mom stood up and went around the table to give him a big kiss before continuing on to kiss and hug everyone.

That night as he lay in bed thinking, before going to sleep, Pete felt a wonderful joy and contentment. The moon was bright and his heart was brighter. "I didn't need money to give mom a gift she loved, after all," he thought. "How good."

Hope

We moved into our townhouse just about two and a half years ago. It's in the Chinatown part of Chicago. They're still tearing down the old houses and building these new ones. They're surprisingly expensive, everyone says, but we're pretty lucky. My dad, Chan Kwai Chang, does really well with his restaurant supply business, so we can afford it.

Dad's a philosopher. Mom's a poet, grandma's a Bodhisattva and my little sister, Siu Wai (Susie) is a sweet, little China doll. Me? I'm still trying to figure out what I am.

I have a great family, though, and that puts me a couple of steps ahead. When I see all the dysfunctional families on TV or sometimes in my friends' houses, I feel really grateful for how functional my family is.

I'm David (Dai Wai) Chan. This whole thing started back when we first moved in. I was thirteen then. I saw how much more room we had than before and right away I knew I was going to get the puppy I'd wanted for so long.

I went to mom and begged and pleaded but she said no. "Susie has allergies, David, you know that," she said.

"But you're giving her allergy shots, vitamins and acupuncture," I protested.

"So far nothing has helped. Please be reasonable," she said.

So I went to dad. He had his tool kit out and there was that intent look on his face that told me he was on a mission, but he stopped to listen to me anyway. My folks are great that way. "Mom won't let me have a puppy because of Susie's allergies. She's tried everything but nothing's worked," I said. "Can you think of anything I can do about it?"

"Mei-Ling has to balance the health, temperaments and interests of everyone in our family," he said. "But you can pray. When we pray, God listens to our prayers and they are answered."

"So you're saying all I can do is pray?" I asked.

"You don't understand the power of prayer. First we should definitely put in our own best efforts. But 'where all else fails — there prayer succeeds,'" he said, and smiled, and went to try to fix the screen door that opened to the back yard.

Prayer. In our house we all believed in a God that was the same one God for all creation, but we also believed that He was called by many names and worshipped in many ways. My parents and Susie and

I were Christian. My grandma was Buddhist. When I called her a Bodhisattva before, I meant that she's one of the wisest, kindest and most wonderful people I've ever known. If my philosopher dad told me to try prayer then I probably should. And maybe my grandma could tell me what prayer would work best.

I went to her part of the house. We were lucky to have a lot of room and she had a whole suite to herself. I knocked lightly and opened the door to her front room. She was sitting cross legged on the floor with her eyes closed. There was jasmine incense burning before the bronze figure of Kwan Yin in the shrine. Gram always says the beautiful, traditional shrine and the scent of burning incense makes her feel peaceful and that helps her quiet her mind.

When I saw she was in meditation I turned to leave, but she opened her eyes and smiled so I stayed.

"David, my sugared plum," she said.

"Honorable Grandmother," I said and bowed.

"Have you been watching those late-night Charlie Chan movies again?" she asked and smiled.

"Why shouldn't I?" I said. "Our name is Chan," and laughed as she pretended to frown at me.

"Really, Gram," I said. "I want a puppy and mom says no because of Susie's allergies. Dad says I should pray. What do you think?"

"God has seen fit to keep a way open at all times for his human children," she said. "Meditation with complete desirelessness will bring one's soul into the bliss of Light and Realization. But if you are in the early stages it is permissible to pray for what you want. If you pray from your heart and what you want is not bad for you or anyone else, God will hear you."

"But Gram, even if He hears me, is there any guarantee He'll give me what I want?"

"Pray and wait, Davy," she said. "Have faith that He who knows all will know best how to fulfill your prayer."

So that night I prayed. And the next and the next for a whole month. Nothing happened. Susie was still sneezing and coughing if anyone's pet dog or cat got too close to her. Mom still said no. She wrote me a poem about it though, because she knew how bad I felt.

If only I could bless
your each wish with a yes.
But though I feel woe,
I simply must say no.
I know that makes you sad,
and, knowing, I feel bad.
Please, dear heart, do try
to keep your spirits high.
Know the Lord above
surrounds you with His Love.

I asked my dad what he thought. "I think you should learn patience, perseverance and faith, Davy," he said. "God knows what is best for all of us. If we trust Him, we can go through our disappointments with the least pain and most good cheer. Everything happens for our highest good. Often when we look back later we can even see how things all worked out to some really good end we never could have imagined by ourselves."

When I asked Gram she said, "I agree with your dad, Davy. We have to surrender our desires to God and trust Him to fulfill them in whatever way is truly best for us. And remember — He really loves us. His Love means our way is one of hope — perfect hope."

It was about six months later that Dr. Joe Chee visited our school and spoke in assembly. He was a veterinarian representing the National Humane Society and he was on a tour around the country asking kids to volunteer at their local Humane Society animal shelters. He had great slides of all the animals the Humane Society had taken care of and helped to find good homes.

I went up to him after his talk was over. He told me his home was in Shiprock, New Mexico and he was Navajo. "We may have had ancestors in common thousands of years ago," he said. "Many people feel that the first Native Americans immigrated here from China. They came overland across the Bering Land Bridge, a piece of land in the Ice Age where the Bering Strait is now."

What a great guy he was. So knowledgeable and interesting and doing such wonderful work to help the animals. I felt proud to think that thousands of years ago our ancestors had quite possibly known each other. I asked him what volunteering was like and he explained that in a no-kill shelter which most of the shelters were, these days, the animals needed exercising and, most of all, play and affection.

I was so impressed by Dr. Chee's talk I went the next afternoon to our local shelter and volunteered. I've been doing it ever since. I love helping with the animals — playing with them, feeding and petting them. In fact, after I'd volunteered there a year or so I decided I wanted to specialize in veterinary medicine in college. It's a real blessing to know what I want to do. Most of the other kids don't have any idea yet.

Then just this afternoon they brought a little collie puppy in. I was supposed to give the new arrivals a bath before putting them into their enclosures. As I started to go to the washing area the puppy stopped, stood up on her hind paws and put her face up as if she wanted to tell me a secret. I put my face down to hers and she gave me a little lick on the cheek. It was so sweet. A sort of puppy kiss. My heart melted; I felt so much love for her.

Just then Ben, the afternoon aide-in-charge came to tell me there was a call for me. He took the collie pup off to wash her and I ran to the phone. I was sort of afraid cause nobody ever calls me here.

It was Mom. "What's up?" I asked.

"I couldn't wait to tell you, Davy," she said. "I've been hoping for a month and this afternoon I found out for sure. Susie's allergy doctor gave her a clean bill of health. All the stuff we've been doing for the last three years has worked. Either that or she's just grown out of it. Anyway she's not allergic to animals any more. If you want a puppy, you can have one."

I thought I'd burst. I thanked Mom for calling and told her just ten minutes before she called I'd met the prettiest, sweetest puppy I'd ever seen.

I went back to the washing room. Ben was just towel-drying her. Her fur was still wet and plastered down all over. When she saw me, she started wriggling and when Ben let go of her, she skittered over the wet floor right to me, shedding drops of water as she ran.

"This animal adores you, Davy," Ben said. "Too bad your mom won't let you take her home."

"That call was my mom," I said. "She said Susie's over her allergies to animals and I can finally have a puppy if I want one."

"So hey, what are you going to name her ?" Ben asked.

"Hope," I answered.

Inside the Closet, Behind the Door

Once a little girl found a little door inside the closet in her bedroom. She tried to open it, but never could and forgot it. One night, as she lay sleeping, the girl was awakened by shouting and banging and loud noises like explosions. Frightened, she thought if only she could hide she would be safe.

She ran to her closet and tried to open the little door within it. To her surprise and relief, the door opened and she went through. She passed through a vast dark sky filled with stars. On the other side of the door there was a different world. But it felt so familiar somehow. There was another bedroom similar to the one she had just left but much nicer. She looked around and saw many beloved things she had somehow forgotten. There was her favorite doll. There, her china tea set. There, her embroidered, rose pink shawl and there, her sky blue sweater. It was so warm, so welcoming, so perfect.

This was her real room. This was her real home. How could she have forgotten this place? This was where she belonged. How had she gotten lost on the other side of the little door?

She didn't care. She was home. She was safe. She would always stay here. She heard muffled noises coming from beyond the closet. It sounded like loud explosions, but she didn't feel frightened at all. She knew she was safe.

She wandered out of this bedroom and found there was a whole household outside it. It was her real house. She recognized, knew and loved everything she saw. She remembered having been here before and how happy she had been then just as she was now. Why had she ever left? She couldn't remember.

She went outdoors. The house stood upon a tall cliff. She could see a perfect robin's egg blue sky with feathery white clouds dancing in every direction. A pristine green lawn with majestic tall pine trees bordering it stretched as far as she could see. Rivers of winding flower gardens with more kinds of flowers than she had ever imagined twined through the emerald grass in which sparkling dewdrops glistened. Here and there, stately oak trees spread their canopies upward caressing the sky and providing secret, shaded spaces of silence beneath their branches. It was all so familiar and so incredibly, enchantingly beautiful.

She walked in wonderment across the lawn to the edge of the cliff, transfixed by the beauty she saw around her. At the bottom of the cliff was a snow-white beach and the luminous ocean glowing from within. Deep azure-blue, crystalline waves formed and broke over and over upon the beach, leaving damp imprints of their being behind them on the sand as they receded. Each wave differed slightly from every other; each sculpted imprint differed also, but the beach itself was a glorious harmony, a work of art reflecting the beauty of God's unity in diversity.

"I am so happy here," she said. "May I stay?" Then she felt a shiver run through her. She felt a shadow cross the sun. For a moment she feared. "May I stay?" she asked again but received no answer.

"Was there something I have forgotten?" she thought. "Was there something somewhere else I was supposed to do?" She wandered back through the yard to the house. She went in and through the house to her bedroom. Why was she going to her room when the sun was shining? Oh, yes, there was something she wanted to do. She went to the closet and opened the door. Within the closet, she saw the little door. "What is happening beyond that little door?" she wondered.

Intense desire to know what was happening in the other world beyond the little door overtook her. "But wait," she thought. "If I leave will I be able to come back here again?"

"Please, please," she prayed, "If I leave will I be able to come back? Will I remember?"

She felt a smile in her thoughts. She felt a sense of peace and love and joy. The sense of love infused a Presence who spoke without words to her deepest self. "Look for me in the other world. Don't forget your home on this side of the door. There is a path that will lead you back here. Remember to seek it and you will find it. But even if you do forget, some day you'll remember. Then, when you long with all your heart to return, I'll bring you back again — I promise."

She was comforted. She opened the little door and stepped through. It was her old room, but it was an entirely different world from that which she had just left. Everything was a mess. Something bad had happened here. The roof had fallen in, and there was trash everywhere.

She stopped. "Wait, wait. There's something I must remember," she thought. "What was it? Was it a dream? Yes. I dreamed of some place beautiful where I was safe and happy. But what has happened here?"

She walked into the living room. There was rubble and dust everywhere. She went from that room into the kitchen.

A man came rushing up to her. "Mrs. Jones, we've been looking everywhere for you."

Mrs. Jones? She looked down at her hands. They were older. They were wrinkled and she wore a wedding ring.

"I'm so sorry about your family," the man said. "It's terrible. The tornado got half the city, not just your house."

"I forgot I was grown-up," she thought. "I thought I was young and safe and happy. My family? Wait, was it all a dream? I was so happy, I was in another place, a beautiful, wonderful place — I forgot I had a family. How could I forget? Keith, my husband, my best friend, my dearest heart's love and Patrick and Roger — my baby boys, my darlings, so grown-up now, so loving, so good. Oh, how can I bear it?"

"Come on Mrs. Jones," the man said, taking her by the arm. "You can't do anything here. You'll be more comfortable at the shelter. You can get something to eat there and some tea."

"But there's something important inside the house," she said, trying to pull away from him and go back in. "There's something I must remember. It's a door, a way to another place, a happier place — if only I could remember...."

"There's nothing you can do here now. Come back tomorrow, if you have to," the man said sympathetically and led her through the wreckage to a van that would drive her to the emergency shelter.

She went along, but all the time she was thinking there was something she had to remember, something really important. Was it a dream? Like the memory of warmth when standing in the cold, it was gone.

The shelter was in a church. She was given a cot — one of many set up in the gymnasium. As she lay down beneath the coarse blanket to sleep, she felt something comforting reach out and enfold her. She smelled lovely flowers. It was a Presence — a Presence who was familiar somehow. The Presence spoke to her. He told her that everything would be alright. She felt like a child held close in a loving mother's embrace. She started to relax, her heart filled with peace and love and hope.

The next morning she woke to a sunny day. The sun streamed in through the gymnasium windows. There was a slight chip in the glass of one window. This chip in the glass refracted the sunshine so that the light turned into a rainbow as it streamed through. The rainbow stretched from the window across the floor and onto her bed.

As she woke, the Presence spoke a poem to her in her mind. As she heard the words, she mentally saw them as if they were written and realized that what she was hearing could be spelled in different ways. It was delightful to realize this and she said the words to herself over and over so she wouldn't forget before she could write them down. She touched the rainbow which lay across her pillow and went to look for something to write with.

She found an old lined tablet and a stub of pencil lying half thrown behind one of the large, black trash cans at the back of the gym. She hurriedly wrote down the words she had heard upon awakening:

> *Promise giver,*
> *Promise maker,*
> *Promise keeper*
> *To dim sleeper.*
> *Promise wake her,*
> *Promise keep her.*
> *No heart break her,*
> *Just be friend her.*
> *Promise tend her,*
> *Heal and mend her.*
> *Promise take her*
> *Starways and back home.*

Was it a message? Why had the Presence said it? What did it mean? Who was the Presence? Why did it give her so much hope, so much peace?

After the breakfast of coffee and toast the Red Cross served, she left the shelter and walked back towards her home. The electric crews had worked all night and all the downed wires had been repaired. Since there was no flooding she was able to go up to her house.

What a wreck — all the windows smashed, all the walls leaning in. The roof was half gone, and the remains of the old oak tree that had fallen on it were still jutting out here and there. She walked up to her front door. How odd that it remained whole, untouched, properly shut, guarding nothing but ruin and grief.

"Miaow."

She looked closer at her house. Did that sound come from inside? She opened the front door and stepped across some trash and rubble. A calico cat with patches of orange and white and black and gray rushed up to her meowing loudly.

"Maggie, Maggie!" she exclaimed, picking the little cat up and hugging her tightly. But Maggie meowed urgently and jumped out of her arms and rushed toward the back of the house, then stopped and came back, meowed again and dashed off, then stopped and stared at her.

"Okay, okay. I'll come with you," she said and followed Maggie back to her old bedroom which had suffered the worst of the storm's damage to the house. When she looked at the wreckage of her old room, she started weeping as tragedy overwhelmed the fragile comfort that the poem and finding Maggie had given her.

Maggie went to the door of the old closet and scratched urgently at it. "What is it, Maggie?" she said and walked over to the closet. "Wait. I remember. There's something inside — something important."

She opened the door and Maggie rushed in to stop

before a little door which she pawed at urgently.

"Now I remember. There's something good behind that little door. I used to go inside it when I was young. But I'm all grown-up now. I could never fit through it." Sitting down before the little door, much, much too big to ever fit through, she started weeping desperately, hopelessly, helplessly.

Then there was a sound. She heard a sound far away that was strangely familiar. Maggie's ears cocked forward. She heard it too. It sounded like ocean waves rolling and breaking upon a far-off shore.

"Why are you crying, girl?"

She felt the Presence speaking to her in her thoughts. He sounded so loving. She replied, "I want to go inside that little door but I'm much, much too big."

"Your mind tells you that you are too big," the Presence said. "In reality you are just the right size. Think with your heart, act with your soul. It's only your mind that will not fit."

Maggie pushed the little door. It opened just a crack. The calico cat raced through. "Maggie, Maggie, wait for me," she cried and hurled herself at the little door with all her heart. It opened before her. As she crossed over, trillions of twinkling, glittering stars danced before her inner vision.

She opened her eyes. It was her old room. Everything she loved was here. She remembered it all so clearly now. How could she have forgotten? She was so happy. She raced out of her room and through the house. Her real home. It was all just as it had always been. It was so beautiful, so sweet, so perfect, so dear.

She ran out to the yard. Yes. It was all as she remembered. She ran to the edge of the cliff. There she saw the ocean and heard the waves breaking on the shore below her. She knew that all of the friends and family she had ever loved were here somewhere, and she thought if she went just around the corner of the house she would find them.

She ran back to the house and raced around the corner. There, just a little way off, two boys and a man were playing catch. As she looked, the ball flew through the air right towards her. One of the boys came running after it. It was Roger!

"Oh, Roger, I thought you were gone," she cried, running up to him and hugging him close.

"Hi, Mom," he said. "Gone where? We're all here, and so are you."

As she looked, the other boy and man came running over to join them. It was Keith and Patrick. Her heart felt so much joy and yet it was so natural, so right. Had it ever really been different?

"Oh, my loves. It's so good to see you." She hugged them and kissed them. It was so good to be with them again. "What are you all doing here?" she asked.

"We're here to learn more about God and Love," Keith said.

"We meditate every day," Patrick said.

"Meditate? What's that?" she asked.

"You'll find out, Mom," Roger said.

"We like it. You will too," Keith said.

She felt so much joy and peace. She knew in her heart that she was finally back where she was supposed to be.

Then, she heard the sound of the ocean's roar as its waves washed up upon the beach. She wanted to go closer to the water and rest there just a minute. "I want to walk over to the ocean front for a minute or two," she told her beloved Keith and dearest, darling boys. "You go on with your game — I'll be right back."

As she looked down onto the shore and the rolling waves breaking upon it, she thought "I'm so happy now. My family is here and I love them so much, but somehow I feel like a little girl again. I don't feel grown-up at all."

She felt the Presence in her mind.

"Why did you take so long to bring me back here?" she asked.

"Was it long?" He said.

"It seemed awfully long," she said. "I forgot this world. I forgot you. It was so different on the other side of the door. It wasn't sweet and blissful like it is here. I wasn't truly happy, but it appeared to be all there was."

The Presence said, "I'm glad you're here."

She said, "I lived a whole lifetime there, but now it seems as if it was all a dream."

There was a shimmer of light like the phosphorescence left in the dark sky at the very end of a burst of fireworks. Then, to her great delight, a cloud of golden light grew solid and surrounded a man dressed all in white. The golden light faded until it was just a line about three inches wide surrounding him like a line in a coloring book.

He looked deeply into her eyes. She felt as if a springtime breeze had blown through wide-open windows in a formerly closed-up house. She felt the breeze clearing away all the leftover traces of dirt, dust and sadness from every nook and cranny of her being. "I'm so glad you found me," she said. "I'm so glad you brought me back to you."

He smiled at her and handed her a narcissus flower. Its simple white petals and golden cup-shaped heart seemed to glow. A rich, intoxicating, spicy-sweet fragrance filled the air around them.

"I always keep my promises," He said.

Afterword

I remember thinking, as a child, that there was something wonderful hiding just behind the everyday appearance of the world I lived in. I used to feel closest to that wonder in places of worship and in nature. Sometimes when the sky was full of lightning and thunder and high winds made the tree branches toss wildly, I felt it near. Sometimes in my grandmother's back yard as sunlight turned the pebbles around her pond into magic gems, and the shadowed caves beneath pine tree branches into temples of mystery, I felt it was just a breath away.

I also felt a lot of unhappiness. Whenever I read a book like *The Secret Garden* in which a child was able to become very happy and live in a wonderful world full of love and enchantment, I always wished with all my heart that I could get into the joyful world of that book and stay there so I could be happy too.

I never stopped searching for some way to experience the wonder I believed must exist and, by great good fortune, I was finally gifted to find it in a simple meditation practice taught today by Sant Rajinder Singh.

This meditation has provided the door into my own secret garden and given me the love and happiness I always longed for. Because of this, I want to share Sant Rajinder Singh's introductory Jyoti meditation with you. Only God's love can heal our broken hearts so, whole-hearted, loved and safe ourselves, we can give love wholeheartedly to whomever we meet. I hope that any person at all who longs to be truly loved and really happy will give this meditation a try and find the warmth and wonder that they long for.

— Sharan Shively

Jyoti Meditation

by Sant Rajinder Singh

[reprinted with permission from SK Publications]

This introductory form of meditation, called Jyoti meditation, can be done by anyone as a science. It can be practiced by anyone of any religion, culture, or age. It is a simple and safe process that does not involve any difficult poses or practices.

To practice this meditation, we can sit in a pose that is most convenient in which we can remain still for the longest possible time. We can sit on a chair, we can sit on the floor, we can sit on a sofa, or we can sit cross-legged or with legs straight. We can sit in any manner. For those who are physically unable to sit, they can even lie down. The reason lying down is not recommended is that it is conducive to falling asleep. The main thing is to meditate wherever we are comfortable.

In whatever pose we adopt, there should be no tension in any part of the body. We should sit in a relaxed pose. Once we select the pose, we should not change it during that meditation sitting. We should remain physically still.

Once we pick a pose, we should close our eyes

very gently, just as we do when going to sleep, and concentrate on seeing what lies in front of us. There should be no pressure on the eyes. Our eyes should be as relaxed as they are when we go to sleep. Since these physical eyes are not those by which we will be seeing the inner realms, there is no need to turn our eyeballs upwards in the hopes that we will see something there. We should not concentrate on the forehead. Instead, we should keep our eyeballs horizontal, a few inches in front of us, as if we were looking straight ahead.

When we close our eyes, we will first see darkness. That which sees the darkness is our inner eye. With the inner eye, we should gaze lovingly, sweetly, and penetratingly into whatever is in front of us. We should be relaxed but attentive, as if we were watching a movie screen and waiting for the movie to begin. This is a process in which we do not worry about the world outside or what is going on in the body below. We are only trying to invert so as to reach the worlds within.

Once we close our eyes and focus our attention in front of us, the mind will distract our concentration with thoughts. We will start thinking about all our problems. We will think about the past, we will think about the present and we will think about the future. It could bring us thoughts about our families or about our friends. Mind has many ways of trying to distract us from sitting in meditation and to keep us from learning about our soul and God.

To provide assistance to help bring the attention to the eye focus and to still the mind, repeat any name of God with which you feel comfortable. If the mind is busy in the repetition of the Name of God, it cannot distract the attention with thoughts. While we gaze into the middle of what lies in front of us, we repeat the Name. We repeat it mentally and not out loud. It is to be repeated slowly, at intervals, not in quick succession. There should be a slight pause between each repetition.

While the repetition goes on mentally, we gaze at the field of darkness lying in front of us. We should not think about the world outside, the body below, or the process of withdrawal of the sensory currents from the body. We should not put any attention on our breathing. Our breathing should go on normally, just as it does when we read, study, work, or move about. As we go about our day-to-day life, we do not think about our breathing.Similarly, in meditation it should go on automatically.

Our job is to sit calmly and quietly and lovingly gaze into the darkness lying in front of us. As we do so, the attention will automatically begin to collect at the single eye, between and behind the two eyebrows. We should just go on repeating the Name of God and gazing.

As we meditate more, as our attention is focused and we progress, we may be able to see inner vistas. We may see flashes of Light or light of any color, inner stars, moon, and sun. Whatever we see we should concentrate in the middle of it. As we sit in meditation we can experience peace, bliss, and joy.

Thank You!

First and foremost, I'd like to thank Sant Kirpal Singh Ji Maharaj, Sant Darshan Singh Ji Maharaj, and Sant Rajinder Singh Ji Maharaj. Thay have transformed my life through their teachings, guidance, meditation, grace, and unconditional love. Because of them there is so much that is good and wonderful in my life that there is no way I could ever express it adequately or thank them enough.

I would also like to thank all the authors whose stories and poems gave me worlds of wonder when I was young; whose stories gave me peers who longed for and searched as I did for things most of the world ignored; whose works entertained and inspired me when I felt most alone; whose works delight and accompany me still. Thanks also to all the people in my life who offered me caring, support and knowledge. I often think of bits of training, teaching, advice, help or kindness but am unable to tell the person who gave it how much I treasure it still.

Special thanks to Kathryn Kruger, Larry Levin, Sam Pletcher, Debbie Purdy, Valerie Tarrant, and Isabel Wolf whose help with this book was invaluable.

Thanks also for help (in whatever form) with this book to: Harriet Beckett, Bette Elizabeth Drew, Mona

Grayson, Ricki Linksman, Joan Morgan, Ellen Nardiello, Hilbert Ng, Irene Schramm, Vinod Sena, Lakshmi Kapoor Willis, and Marshall Zaslove.

About the Author

Sharan Shively grew up in the Ohio woodlands. She loved to read all the works of mythology, fairy tales and fantasy she could find.

She has a degree in art and English and has worked as a teacher, writer and editor.

She has studied meditation and love-in-action or positive ethical values for thirty years under the guidance of Sant Kirpal Singh, Sant Darshan Singh, and Sant Rajinder Singh, making numerous trips to India to visit their Ashrams.

She currently lives in Illinois with her two cats in a small cottage between two lakes. In the lake to the west, every evening, the setting sun is reflected. In the lake to the east, every morning, the rising sun's reflection can be seen as it shines forth to greet the world again.

Prayer for Beauty, Peace, Love and Light

Forgive your past and dream into the Light.
Our past makes us what we are.
Our dreams make us what we will be.

May we walk in beauty.
With beauty above us,
with beauty below us,
with beauty beside us,
and beauty all around us.

May we live in peace.
With peace above us,
with peace below us,
with peace beside us,
and peace all around us.

May love enfold us.
With love above us,
with love below us,
with love beside us,
and love all around us.

May all Light guide us.
Light above us,
Light below us,
Light beside us,
and Light within us,
until we reach our Home.